Charlotte Phillips has been reading romantic fiction since her teens, and she adores upbeat stories with happy endings. Writing them for Mills & Boon® is her dream job. She combines writing with looking after her fabulous husband, two teenagers, a four-year-old and a dachshund. When something has to give, it's usually housework. She lives in Wiltshire.

Other Modern Tempted™ titles by Charlotte Phillips:

THE PLUS-ONE AGREEMENT

**This and other books by Charlotte Phillips
are available in eBook format
from www.millsandboon.co.uk**

DEDICATION

For Sam, who keeps me smiling
when I think I'm rubbish. I am so proud of you.

THE FLAT IN NOTTING HILL

Love and lust in the city that never sleeps!

Izzy, Tori and Poppy are living the London dream—sharing a big flat in Notting Hill, they have good jobs, wild nights out…and each other.

They couldn't be more different, but one thing is for sure: when they start falling in love they're going to be very glad they've got such good friends around to help them survive the rollercoaster…!

THE MORNING AFTER THE NIGHT BEFORE
by Nikki Logan

SLEEPING WITH THE SOLDIER
by Charlotte Phillips

YOUR BED OR MINE?
by Joss Wood

ENEMIES WITH BENEFITS
by Louisa George

Don't miss this fabulous new continuity from Modern Tempted™!

Dear Reader

Well, here we are again—but this time I'm part of a team! This is the first book I've ever written in collaboration with other authors, and I hope you have as much fun reading it as I did planning and writing it.

Writing is usually very solitary—just me and my laptop—but with this book I've had three other fab authors to brainstorm and chat with. We shared photos and decor plans for the flat in Notting Hill, and bounced around ideas for the café where all the flatmates meet up.

The best bit has been seeing glimpses of Lara and Alex in the other books in *The Flat in Notting Hill* series. For once the road to happy-ever-after for my couple isn't the limit of their story, and I can see a bigger picture of their friendships and their lives together. Add to that the wonderful vibrancy of the Notting Hill setting and this story really leapt off the page for me. I hope it does for you too!

Love

Charlotte x

SLEEPING WITH THE SOLDIER

BY
CHARLOTTE PHILLIPS

First published in Great Britain 2014
by Mills & Boon, an imprint of Harlequin (UK) Limited,
Eton House, 18-24 Paradise Road, Richmond, Surrey, TW9 1SR

© 2014 Harlequin Books S.A.

Special thanks and acknowledgement are given to Charlotte Phillips
for her contribution to *The Flat in Notting Hill* series.

ISBN: 978-0-263-24295-9

Harlequin [...] that are natural,
renewable [...] and made from wood grown in
sustainable [...] manufacturing processes conform
to the lega[l ...] of the country of origin

Printed an[d ...] in Great Britain
by CPI An[...]ham, Wiltshire

CHAPTER ONE

LARA CONNOR WAS aiming to corner the rich Notting Hill market in boutique lingerie and she wasn't about to achieve that heady dream with French knickers that looked as if a club-fingered chimp had sewn them together.

She stared in disbelief at the mass of pale pink silk and delicate lace now rucked up in a tangle of mad stitches beneath the foot of her sewing machine and gritted her teeth hard enough to make her jaw ache. Above her head the banging started again with a new urgency that really brought out the hostility in her.

She liked to think she was a glass-half-full kind of person, laid-back, live and let live, default mood: happy. But the noise pollution emanating from the flat above all night, every night, had meant her sleep had been broken for weeks now. Tiredness had pushed her normally sunny attitude to the brink of her patience and, frankly, if it didn't stop now, murder might be on the cards.

She lifted the foot of the machine, disentangled the ball of expensive fabric from the needle and examined it. Beyond saving. She lobbed it across the room into the 'remnants' bin. The knickers weren't even salvageable enough to go into the 'seconds' bin. And having sunk every penny into this venture, she couldn't afford to keep slipping up like this. The 'remnants' bin was looking far too full for her liking, and it was all the fault of the Lothario upstairs, who apparently couldn't let a day pass by without getting laid.

The clanking and banging in the pipes had begun a few weeks ago, not long after Lara had moved in. The sudden increase in noise coincided with the return of the soldier brother of Poppy, who owned the flat upstairs. Lara had got to know Poppy quite well over the last four or five weeks, and her flatmate, Izzy. A brief hello on the stairs had quickly progressed to coffee and chat in the downstairs café. Both girls were excited to hear about Lara's lingerie designs. Izzy had even bought a couple of samples. On her own in a new place, Lara was especially pleased to have made friends. If only Poppy's brother could have a *smidge* of her consideration.

Sitting in Ignite, the ground-floor café, while Lara updated her blog courtesy of the free Wi-Fi, she'd picked up plenty of gossip from the other old-fire-station residents about Alex. He was rumoured to be some military hero, honourably discharged from the army after frontline action abroad. The building was also awash with gossip about his endless stream of women; the word was that he bedded a different one every night! And two or three times she'd actually seen said women, sporting that giveaway combination of evening clothes, bed hair and smug smile, making the walk of shame when she'd nipped down to the café for a takeaway coffee first thing in the morning. Lara had watched pityingly; she couldn't think of anything more pointless. With all this evidence taken as a whole, there was no real question as to the source of the noise pollution that was tiring her out, disrupting her work and thus costing her money, of which she had absolutely no more.

The first couple of times it might even have been funny. His bed must be shoved right up against the radiator, because the water pipes for the top flat were clearly shared by her own little studio flat below. At first she'd rolled her eyes in exasperation and—possibly—a hint of wistful envy. Not that it had anything to do with the military hero himself, of course; in her opinion he sounded far too attractive for his own good. But still, it had been a long time since she'd last seen any action in that department. That was what big aspirations did to your life. There had to be sacrifices; something had to give. Lara Connor had plans and ambitions, and she intended to keep her eye on the prize.

The next step on that journey to success was the small shop she'd managed to secure in Notting Hill for the next two months. Her own pop-up shop to showcase her own line of vintage-inspired lingerie. The rent on this little flat was extortionate and had eaten away at her savings, but it was worth it so she could live near the premises and she'd been working all the hours she could muster. Sewing was only a part of it—there was marketing to think of, the shop to fit and decorate. Night and day her mind was filled with nothing else. She was already exhausted, just with the workload she had to shoulder, but she cared about none of it because this was the next step in her game plan, from which she would not be distracted.

Certainly not by some inconsiderate love god living upstairs. The endless noise was beginning to jeopardise her carefully laid plans, and she quite simply was not going to stand for it any longer. Especially since it now seemed that all night was no longer adequate for his needs. This morning she'd heard the familiar slam of the door as his most recent conquest left the building. But this time it hadn't been followed by the welcome peace that she needed to produce the intricate lingerie she designed herself to the exacting standards she demanded. She worked with delicate, fine fabrics. Silks, lace, ribbons, velvet. The kind of garments she made took skill and close attention to detail. Absolute concentration was required.

Instead, what she'd had was half an hour of mad hammering. For the first few minutes she'd tried to ignore it, waiting to see if one of the other residents would intervene. Surely she couldn't be the only one driven mad by this? But as the minutes ticked by and the noise didn't abate she came to realise that clearly no one else *was* around to intervene. They'd all gone out to work, of course, while work for Lara took place right here. She needed to concentrate on her sewing. Everything was riding on this stock being perfect. Seconds were not an option.

As she pushed her chair back grimly and grabbed her door key from the table the bashing overhead began again in earnest, bringing a fresh wave of anger to bubble up inside her.

All night, every night was one thing. Was she now expected to put up with this racket all day too?

Enough was enough.

Shoulders squared, teeth gritted, she took the stairs up to the top floor grimly, ready to give Poppy's inconsiderate brother a piece of her sleep-deprived mind, and the planned outburst screeched to a halt on the tip of her tongue as she rounded the corner at the top of the stairs. The hinge on her jaw seemed to be suddenly loose.

Poppy's inconsiderate brother?

Correction: Poppy's all but naked, roped with muscle, fit and breathtakingly gorgeous soldier hero brother. His modesty was saved only by a very small white towel, which was held up on his muscular hips by a single fold. Hard muscle twined the tanned biceps and broad shoulders. His stomach was drum-tight and his short dark hair was damply tousled. Smoothly tanned skin gave away the fact he'd spent months abroad in action before coming here. By sheer will she fixed her eyes above his neck when all they wanted to do was dip lower and check out those perfect abs.

And OK, for a moment she *might* have been stunned into silence by the revelation that, actually, the rumours were true, Poppy's brother really *was* drop-dead gorgeous, and by the fact that his modesty was hidden by the tiniest of white towels, but then he'd gone on to ruin the effect by raising his clenched fist and hammering on the closed door of the flat, reproducing the sound that had driven her to the edge of her sanity for the past half an hour. Up close it was monstrously loud and her already aching head throbbed in protest.

'I think,' she snapped, in the coldest voice she could muster, 'we can safely assume that everyone who lives on the other side of that door is either out or deaf.'

Alex Spencer stopped, knuckles poised mid-hammer, and turned sideways to look at her. Her thick blond hair was piled up messily on her head with a pencil stuck through the middle of it, she had a full rosebud mouth, and wide china-blue eyes that would have been captivating if they hadn't got an expression in them that implied she'd quite like to see him decomposing in a ditch. She wore a pale pink cardigan with the top two buttons undone, revealing a silky smooth expanse of flawless porcelain décolletage, cropped jeans and bare feet. And even though he was so tired he could hardly see straight, and not only because he'd just spent a very active night in bed that involved anything but sleep, his pulse managed a jolt of interest.

'And you are…?' he said, raising sarcastic eyebrows as if she were the one who looked out of place and it were perfectly normal to be walking the corridors wearing a bath towel.

'The poor sap who lives downstairs,' she snapped. '*Directly* downstairs, to be specific. Right below *you*.'

He stared at her, his tired brain struggling to process what she was saying. It felt as if he were thinking through a very large wad of cotton wool. Technically, thanks to the way his sickening insomnia had progressed, night time for him had pretty much now turned into day and vice versa. Thus it was currently an hour or so past his bedtime and his patience was balanced on a knife edge.

'What are you talking about?'

The question opened the floodgates and he took a defensive step backwards.

'Your night-time action is ruining my *life*,' she wailed. 'All night, every night, crashing and clanking pipes while you get your rocks off with whatever girl you happen to have brought back. Your bed must be right up against the radiator or something. The noise travels down the pipes and echoes round my bedroom as if I'm in the bloody room with you. It's utter selfishness! I can hear *every move you make* and I can't take it anymore!' She raised her hands up and pressed them to the sides of her head as if she thought it might explode. 'I can't *have* this kind of distraction. I've only got a week or so left before the shop launches and I'm going to go crazy if I don't get some uninterrupted *sleep*.'

The blue eyes took on a hint of madness, and an unexpected twinge of sympathy twisted his stomach because restful sleep was currently an elusive thing for him too. It had been since he'd returned from his recent overseas tour via the hospital. He'd worked his way through convalescence at breakneck speed after the chest injuries he'd sustained in a roadside bomb, only to learn that he wouldn't be going back. Physical injury was one thing, an early end to his career was quite another. Discharge from the army had not been what he wanted, no matter that it was honourable. He had a lot on his mind, he kept telling himself—it was no wonder that he didn't sleep like a baby at night.

'The shop?' he said.

'I'm in the middle of launching a pop-up shop in Portobello Road. It's my first try at moving into proper retail instead of market stalls. I need it to be a success and *nothing's* going to stop me, including your libido!'

Her angry explanation of her business commitments brought a lurching reminder that currently his own life was cruising along rudderless. It wasn't as if he had a direction right now, or plans to consider. Lack of sleep had no consequence in *his* life, aside from the fact that his routine was getting a bit out of kilter, and who really cared about that? Since his social circle currently consisted of a group of girly flatmates, an old friend who was hardly ever there, and his kid sister, concern about his sleep pattern wasn't exactly a buzzing topic of conversation. And since his sleep problems were rooted in an unrelenting spate of cold-sweat nightmares that made staying awake through the dark hours extremely attractive, he'd quite like to keep it that way.

After operations to remove shrapnel and four months of medical care, his physical recovery was as complete as it was going to get. He'd worked hard to regain his fitness, thinking that would be an end to it, believing he'd got off lightly. He hadn't counted on the nightmares continuing. He hadn't told anyone about them, not even Poppy, vaguely thinking that verbalising their existence might somehow give them even more of a grip on him. Easier to just evade sleep and hope they would subside. To help things along, he filled his waking hours with distracting activity, taking full advantage of the sudden lack of discipline and routine in his life after years of moulding to the requirements first of boarding school and then the armed forces.

The sense of purpose and the camaraderie that he'd come to take for granted in the army left a gaping hole in his life now it was unexpectedly gone. Hence the appeal of filling his time with far less challenging distractions. For the first time in his life he'd thrown himself into having fun, losing all sense of his current pointless existence by bedding as many women as possible. It wasn't difficult. Women seemed to fall at his feet with minimal effort on his part, just the way they always had done.

Except, possibly, for this one.

'If this carries on I'll report you to the local council for noise pollution,' she was snarling. 'Can't you phone Poppy?'

He cast exasperated hands down at himself in the small towel.

'With what, exactly? Do I look like I've got a phone

stashed on my person? If my sister would just haul herself out of her pit and *answer the bloody door*, I wouldn't *need* to be making any noise,' he yelled at the closed door, pressing his point by adding in another quick bash on it, which made the crazy neighbour from downstairs stiffen like a meerkat.

'Will you *stop* with the knocking?' she hollered. 'Is Poppy deaf?'

'Not as far as I'm aware.'

'Then she's not bloody *in there*, is she? You've been hammering on that door for half an hour and it's loud enough to wake the dead.' She threw her hands up in a gesture of exasperation. 'For Pete's sake, she must be at *work*. I saw her the other day and she mentioned she was on call this week.'

The implications of that information burst through his mind in a flurry of exasperation. Poppy could be gone for hours and he couldn't bring himself to interrupt her work as a medic for something as ludicrously embarrassing as locking himself out. Her flatmate, Izzy, had just moved out and the only other person with a key was his friend Isaac, who was supposedly crashing in the extra room but who actually spent more time away than he did at home. He was currently globetrotting between swanky new potential continental venues for his chain of cocktail bars.

He had to face facts. He could hang out in the hallway in a towel for a chunk of the day until Poppy got back. Or he could sweet-talk the interfering neighbour, who looked as if she'd be glad to see his head on a spike.

He stepped away from the door, anticipating that an apology might not have quite the clout it needed if he was still within hammering distance of it.

He spread his hands.

'Look, I'm sorry. What's your name?'

She narrowed suspicious eyes at his newly amenable tone.

'Lara Connor.'

'Lara. I'm Alex.'

She nodded at him, not a hint of a smile, so he tried a bit harder, attempting to mould his face into an apologetic expression.

'I'm sorry for the noise. The *disruption*. I had no idea I was bothering anyone. It's not as if anyone else has complained.'

Quite the opposite. The biggest problem he had was wriggling out of any follow-up dates. He had absolutely no desire to ruin what was a very nice distraction plan by bringing anything so emotionally demanding as a proper *relationship* into the situation.

As apologies went it was all a bit pants in Lara's opinion.

'Why *would* anyone else complain? No one else has a bed directly below yours,' she said. 'And I don't need an apology or a load of rubbish excuses. What I really want is some kind of assurance that you'll make an effort and stop the racket.'

'I'll move my bed away from the wall,' he conceded. His voice was clipped and very British. She noticed he didn't offer to interrupt the endless flow of women through his bedroom.

'Right,' she said. 'And what about now? You can't keep hammering on that door—my sanity is hanging by a thread. What are you going to do until Poppy gets back?'

She folded her arms and frowned at him.

He shrugged resignedly.

'I'll just have to wait it out. Unless you'd like to take pity on me.'

'I don't think so,' she said, smoothing her hair back from her face.

'It could be hours.' His expression took on a pitiful look. 'I don't even have a jacket.'

'Tough,' she said. 'It'll do you good to put up with a bit of discomfort for a change.' She made a move towards the stairs, wondering how far he might go with the grovelling, enjoying the upper hand. She'd let him suffer a bit longer and then offer to let him wait in her flat.

His grovelling had apparently reached its limit. Silence as she descended the top step and then a sudden flurry of bangs on the door started up again. She turned back to him incredulously.

He shrugged, his upraised knuckles poised at chest level.

'You know, I'm really not *convinced* Poppy isn't in there,' he said. 'Maybe if I knock long enough, she might show.'

He put enormous emphasis on the words 'long enough', making it crystal clear he was prepared to knock all day if necessary.

Anger bubbled hotly through her as she stared at him, seeing the challenge in his eyes and knowing that if she wanted to get any work done today at all she would have to give on this. It was all she could do to force herself to act rationally, when what she wanted to do was snarl at him like a fishwife. She would give on this because it was in her best interest, thereby retaining the upper hand rather than dragging herself down to his level, but he needn't think this was over. Not for *one moment*.

'Come on, then,' she said, turning back towards the wrought-iron staircase.

She glanced around to see him looking after her. The few paces extra distance would have given her an eye-wateringly fantastic full body view of him if she hadn't bitten her lip in her determination to keep her eyes fixed from the neck up.

'What?'

'I give in. You win. I've got more important things to do than stand here arguing with you. You can use my phone if you want to try and get hold of Poppy.' The words stuck in her craw because she really didn't *need* a half-naked ex-soldier blagging his way into her flat when she had a mountain of silk knickers with velvet ribbons and frills to sew on the back. 'I haven't got her work number, but you must know it, right? Or I think I've got Izzy's number somewhere. Maybe we can get her to drop by if she still has a key. You can wait in my flat if you like,' she added grudgingly.

She led the way down the wrought-iron stairs before he could say anything triumphant. If he did that she might be tempted to call the police.

CHAPTER TWO

ALEX FOLLOWED HER down the narrow stairwell and into her flat, and, if he'd thought a few bras hanging over the bathtub in Poppy's flat was a girly step too far, this was a whole new ballgame.

There was an enormous clothes rail directly opposite, stuffed to breaking point with clothes. And not just any clothes. Everything seemed to be made of silk, satin, lace and velvet. Subtle pinks and creams hung alongside vampy deep reds, peacock blues and purples. There were spools of silk and velvet ribbon in every colour imaginable. In one corner of the room was a headless mannequin wearing a black silky bra with tassels along the cups and matching knickers. He stared at it for an incredulous moment. Rolls of fabric were stacked against the wall and hung over the back of the sofa in the corner and the room was dominated by an enormous trestle table with two different kinds of sewing machine on it.

'Is it just you living here?' he asked as she crossed the cramped room to the kitchen area at the other end. He was used to Poppy's roomy flat. This was a shoebox in comparison.

She nodded.

'It's a one-bed studio. There isn't much space but it's

in such a perfect location for my shop. The time I'm saving by living so close kind of makes the lack of space worth it.' She nodded towards the sofa. 'Have a seat. I'll make some tea.'

'And what exactly is it that you do?' he said, picking his way through the clutter to the overstuffed sofa. It was covered in a brightly coloured patchwork throw and he had to move a huge pile of silk and lace remnants before there was room to sit down.

She was clattering about in the tiny kitchen area in the corner. There was a doorway at the side of the room with a length of some filmy cream fabric hanging across it as a curtain. He narrowed his eyes, trying to get his bearings. Her bedroom must be down there on the right if it really was situated underneath his, as she claimed. He shook his head lightly because he had absolutely zero interest in how she spent her nights.

This was a means to an end, nothing more, a marginal step up from waiting it out in the hallway upstairs. He had no desire whatsoever to find out more about the infuriating woman from downstairs. He sank onto the sofa, shifted to one side uncomfortably and tugged out a pale pink feather boa from underneath him. For Pete's sake.

'I design and make my own line of boutique lingerie,' she said.

It was impossible to miss the faint trace of pride in her voice.

'Knickers, camisoles, nightgowns, slips, bustiers, basques. You name it.' She counted them off on her fingers. 'Vintage inspired, Hollywood glamour, that kind of thing. I like to make the most of the female figure.'

His mind reeled a little. She might as well have been speaking in some foreign language and he'd felt enough of a fish out of water already in the past couple of weeks, thank you very much. After living at close quarters with soldiers for the best part of the last few years, much of that time in the roughest of conditions, moving in with a group of girls was like living with a gaggle of aliens. Everything was scented. *Everything.* There was girly underwear hanging over the radiators. The fridge was full of hummus, low-fat yogurt and other hideous foodstuffs that filled him with distaste, the topics of conversation mystified him and the bathroom was full of perfumed toiletries. He'd grabbed the opportunity when Poppy's friend Izzy had moved rooms a few weeks ago to draft in male back-up in the form of his old schoolfriend Isaac, but in reality it had made little difference because Isaac was hardly ever there. Alex was out of his depth as it was, and now he was catapulted into a room full of lingerie.

'I've been selling from market stalls for ages now, building up a customer base,' Lara was saying. 'And I have a blog—*"Boudoir Fashionista".*' She made a frame in the air with her hands as if imagining the title on a shop sign.

'A blog?' he repeated. The conversation was becoming more surreal by the minute. He leaned his head back against the sofa. His headache seemed to be intensifying.

'Mmm…' She continued to clatter about in the kitchen, not turning round. 'I showcase my lingerie, blog about fashion and beauty. I've been wanting to expand the business for a while, try my hand at retail, but it's such a gamble in terms of cost, you have no idea. And then I started looking into pop-up shops.'

He didn't answer. Her voice was sweet, melodic even, pleasant to listen to. He closed his heavy eyes to ease the thumping headache, a side effect of his crazy off-kilter sleep pattern that seemed to be becoming a regular thing.

'It's just a short-term thing, so less risk. There are places that advertise opportunities. You take on empty premises, sometimes even just for a day. I couldn't believe it when I found the place on Portobello Road—it was like a dream. I've got it for the next couple of months. Perfect timing for me to take advantage of the run up to Christmas and long enough to see if I can make it work.'

Lara gave the tea a final stir. Busying herself in the kitchen was an autopilot way of taking her mind off how much tinier the already minuscule flat suddenly felt with him in it. Small it might be but it had still been at the absolute limit of what she could afford. Desperate to give everything to the pop-up shop opportunity, she'd quickly realised that living nearby would be a huge advantage. Failure was absolutely *not* an option.

She'd give him the tea and then try to track down Izzy. The thought of having him here under her feet all day made her stomach feel squiggly. She had *tons* of work to do and she'd lost nearly an hour this morning already to first his noise and now the follow-up chaos. She didn't have *time* to step in as rescue party for neighbours. She turned back to cross the room to him. Three paces in and she came to a stop, smile fading from her face, mug of tea in each hand.

He was fast asleep.

He looked completely out of place among the frills, ribbons and lace that festooned the sofa. He had the most tightly honed muscular physique she'd ever seen outside a glossy fashion magazine, his shoulders were huge, his abs perfectly defined. One huge hand rested against his chiselled jaw as if he'd been propping his chin up when he nodded off.

She watched him for a moment. In sleep the defensive expression on his face when he'd given her his half-arsed apology for the noise was nowhere to be seen. The dark hair was dry now, the short cut totally in keeping with his military background; she could easily imagine him in uniform. The face below was classically handsome. His cheekbones were sharply defined, followed up with a firm jawline and strong mouth. Her eyes roamed lower and she caught her breath in surprise.

The upstairs landing was pretty shadowy and he'd been turned away from her for much of the time. Add in the fact that she'd been making a heroic effort to keep her eyes from wandering below his neckline and as a result she only now got a proper view of his body. A twist of sympathy surged through her.

The left-hand side of the tautly muscled chest was heavily puckered and ruched with a web of scar tissue. She pressed her lips together hard. Of course she'd heard from Poppy that Alex had been injured in action but, having heard and seen the evidence of his sexual prowess, she'd assumed whatever had happened to him must have been pretty minor.

Whatever had happened to cause that scarring could most certainly *not* be pretty minor.

She put the two mugs down on the edge of the sewing table and moved closer to him, hand outstretched towards his shoulder to shake him gently awake, and then her eyes stuttered over the shadows beneath the dark eyelashes. He looked exhausted, and no wonder. From what she knew of him, he barely ever slept. His breathing now was rested and even. She withdrew her hand.

Why not let him sleep? Yes, she could try and contact Izzy or Poppy, but really she'd wasted enough time today already on this situation.

She tugged the multi-coloured patchwork throw from the side of the sofa. Her foster mother had made it for her and it was deliciously huge and comforting to snuggle into. She tucked it gently over him. He didn't even stir.

Five minutes later and she had her own mug of tea at her elbow as she got back to her sewing. She had the finishing touches to do on fifty-odd pairs of silk knickers. And that was just for starters.

It felt as if hours had passed when a moan of distress made her foot slip from the pedal of the sewing machine. She'd been so engrossed in her work that she'd almost forgotten she had a house guest. The room had grown dark now in the late afternoon; the small light from the sewing machine and the angled lamp above her workspace were the only sources of light. She stood up and looked curiously at Poppy's brother, sprawled in the shadows on the sofa. Deciding she must have imagined it, she moved to sit back down.

He twisted in his sleep.

She frowned. Abandoning her chair, she took a step towards him. His hands were twisting in the throw she'd draped over him and he let out another cry. Almost a shout this time, enough to make her jump. She watched his face as it contorted. Sympathy twisted in her stomach as she caught sight again of his scarred chest in the dim light. Where was he right now in his mind? In the middle of some hideous battle?

His body twisted sharply again and she couldn't stand

it any longer. She reached out to shake him awake, to take him away from whatever horror he was reliving.

First there was the vague impression of something stroking his upper arm. Tentative, not rough. And then there was the scent, something clean and flowery, like roses. It reminded Alex vaguely of his mother's dressing room back at their country home, with its antique dressing table and ornate perfume bottles and he flinched at the thought. It had been years since he'd visited the family home and he had absolutely no plans to do so in the foreseeable future. Why would he? For a place filled on and off with so many people, so many offshoots of the family, it had been bloody lonely for a kid.

He opened his eyes, disorientation making his mind reel.

He struggled to place himself in a panic. Not his army quarters. And not his room in his sister's flat, with its calming military organisation. Instead he was in a room that could only really be described as a *boudoir*. And it was getting dark.

He struggled to his feet, his mind whirling. Of course, he'd been locked out of Poppy's flat and the downstairs neighbour had offered to make him tea. That was the last thing he remembered. He looked down at himself as the quilt covering him fell away and saw that the towel around his hips was hanging askew. He snatched it closed again. Horrified, he realised he'd been sleeping here in a stranger's flat with his scars on show for her to view at her leisure.

The blonde neighbour was standing a few feet away, an expression of concern on her pretty face. The sewing machine was lit up on the desk by a bright angled lamp. A neatly folded pile of pink silk lay further down the table. A tentative smile touched the corners of her rosebud mouth.

'Are you OK?' she asked. 'You were…' a light frown touched her eyebrows '…calling out in your sleep.'

The heat of humiliation began at his neck and climbed burningly upwards as he regained a grip on reality. He'd had a nightmare. In full view of her. Had he shouted? What had he said? How could he have been so stupid as to let himself fall asleep here?

'What time is it?' he managed, rubbing a hand through his hair as if it might somehow help to clear his foggy head.

'Nearly six,' she said. 'I was just about to wake you. Poppy's home, I think—I heard her go up the stairs to the flat. So you should be able to get back in now.'

Six?

He'd slept the entire day. He avoided her eyes. What must she *think* of him, just falling asleep like that? And then having a bad dream, like some kid. He couldn't quite believe that he could relax enough to fall asleep in a strange place with a strange person. His tiredness must be a lot more ingrained than he'd thought it was.

'I can't believe I fell asleep,' he blustered. 'You should have woken me.'

'I couldn't really believe it either,' she said. 'Of course *I* think my business plan is the most interesting topic of discussion on the planet.' She smiled. 'But it made you nod off in the space of about ten minutes.'

He shook his head. What the hell must she be thinking?

'I'm sorry.'

'It's a *joke*,' she said, making a where's-your-sense-of-humour? face. 'I'm joking?'

'Right,' he said. Awkwardness filled the room, making it feel heavy and tense. He had to get out of here.

'I *was* going to wake you,' she said, 'but I didn't have the heart.'

'Oh, really?' He zeroed in on that comment. Was this some kind of sympathy vote because she'd seen his awful scars? Or worse, because he'd cried out in his sleep? He didn't do sympathy. And he didn't do bursts of emotion either. Nearly thirty years in the stiff-upper-lip environment of his military-obsessed family did that for a person. Stoicism was essential. His father had made that pretty damn clear when Alex was just a kid, an attitude later reinforced at boarding school and then in the army. Emotion was something you stamped on, definitely not something to be expressed among strangers.

'You looked so peaceful,' she went on. 'And you've clearly been getting hardly any sleep if your noise pollution is anything to go by.'

There was an edge to her voice that told him she was still narked about that. He didn't let it penetrate, there was no need to, since he had absolutely no intention of running into her again after today.

'Cup of tea?' she asked him. 'Your last one got cold. Are you sure you're OK?'

He shook his head, automatically folding the enormous throw and placing it neatly at the side of the sofa. He had no idea how she could live in such a cluttered room without going mad. It jarred his military sense of order.

'I am perfectly fine,' he snapped. 'And I've taken up

enough of your time. Now I know Poppy's back I'll get out of your way.'

He headed for the door as she watched him, a bemused expression on the pretty face.

'Bye, then,' he heard her call after him as he pulled the door shut.

A thank-you might have been nice.

Then again, she didn't have time for niceties. Neither did she give a stuff as long as Alex curbed the disruptive noise from upstairs.

Forty-eight hours had now passed with a definite reduction in noise levels although she'd seen no corresponding drop in the stream of disposable girls visiting. That was the thing about working from home for all waking hours—the comings and goings of other residents in the building amounted to distractions, and she couldn't fail to notice them. He must have moved his bed away from the radiator because the endless clanking had ceased. Not, of course, that she was dwelling on Alex Spencer's bedroom activities.

What mattered was that normal sleep quality had been resumed and thank goodness, because the launch of the shop was only a week away now. Just time to fit in a quick shower this morning and then she would head over there to add a few more finishing touches to the décor before she began to move stock in. She'd managed to track down a beautiful French-style dressing screen, the kind you might find in a lady's bedroom, gorgeously romantic. No run-of-the-mill changing cubicles for her little shop. Still, she wanted to try it out in different positions until she found the perfect location for it.

She rubbed shampoo into her hair, closing her eyes

against the soap bubbles and running through a mental list of the hundred-plus things she needed to get done today. A full-length gilt-framed mirror had been delivered the previous day; it would provide the perfect vintage centrepiece for the small shop floor, and she needed to decide where best to put that too. Then there were garlands of silk flowers to hang and some tiny white pin lights to add to the girly atmosphere she wanted to achieve.

The torrent of water rinsing through her hair seemed to be losing its force. She opened one eye and squinted through the bubbles up at the shower head. Yep. The usual nice flow was definitely diminishing. And without the sound of the running water she was suddenly able to hear a monstrous clanking noise coming from behind the wall and above her head.

'What the hell…?' she said aloud as the water reduced to little more than a trickle. The clanking built to a crescendo.

Oh, just bloody *perfect*. Naked, covered in bubbles and with her hair a bird's nest of shampoo, she climbed out of the shower unit and wrapped a towel around her. A quick twist of the sink tap gave a loud clanking spurt of water followed by nothing. She grabbed her kimono from the hook on the back of the bathroom door and shrugged it on as she took the few paces to the kitchen to check the water pressure there.

She didn't make it as far as the sink. Horrified shock stopped her in her tracks as she took in the torrent of water pouring down the wall of the living room, pooling into a flood and soaking merrily into a pile of silk camisoles she'd left in a stack on the floor.

'No-o-o!' she squawked, dashing across the floor,

picking up armfuls of her lovingly made garments and moving them to safety on the other side of the room. She kicked the metal clothes rail out of the way as she passed it, the few garments hanging at one end already splashed by the ensuing torrent of water.

She rushed to the cabinet under the sink, found the stopcock and turned off the water supply as she tried madly to rationalise what could have happened, then she stood, hand plastered to her forehead as her mind worked through the implications of all this. Some of her garments had been soaked through—there went hours of work down the drain. The water continued to spread across the floor in a slow-moving pool. She knew instinctively from the clanking in the pipes that this wasn't going to be some five-minute do-it-yourself quick-fix job. The building was ancient. Behind the glossy makeover of the flat conversion was interlinked original pipework. That much was obvious from the racket they made when the love god upstairs was entertaining.

She had absolutely no money to spare for a plumber. She wondered if any of the rest of the building was affected. Surely it wasn't just her? In a panic she opened the flat door with the intention of knocking on the door opposite and instead ran smack into Poppy, who was on her way up to her own flat with a chocolate croissant in one hand and a takeaway coffee in the other. Poppy's mouth fell open at her insane appearance.

'What the hell happened to you?'

'My flat's flooded,' Lara gabbled. 'It's like the deck of the sodding *Titanic* in there. I've got a shedload of stock in the room, my shop launches next week and I've got no hot water.'

Poppy didn't so much as flinch. She exuded utter calm.

Maybe it was a side-effect of medical training that you simply became good in any crisis. Lara shifted from one foot to the other while she leaned around her to see into the living room.

'Have you turned off the water?'

Lara nodded.

'It seems to have stopped it getting any worse. But just look at the mess.'

Poppy walked into the room and put her coffee down on the trestle table.

'I see what you mean,' she said, peering at the enormous spreading puddle on the floor and the piles of silk and velvet clothing now strewn haphazardly on the other side of the room.

'I need this room to work in and now I'll be behind with my stock levels,' Lara wailed.

The full implications of the situation began to sink in. She'd been running at her absolute limit to get the pop-up shop off the ground in so many ways, working all hours, hocked to the eyeballs financially, using her living accommodation as workspace. She had absolutely no back-up plan. Despair made her stomach churn sickly and she clutched at her hair in frustration. It felt matted and sticky from the puddle of shampoo she'd been unable to rinse out.

'Not to mention the lack of running water,' she added. 'I'll have to stick my head under the tap in the café toilets downstairs.'

'You rent, don't you?' Poppy said, unruffled, crossing the room to look at the huge dark patch on the wallpaper. 'Have you called the landlord?'

Lara sat down on the sofa and put her head in her

hands. She'd been far too busy having a meltdown of major proportions to do anything as practical as that.

'Not yet.'

'It will be down to the landlord to get it sorted, not you. You don't need to stress about cost.'

That was lucky, because *cost* was one thing she really couldn't do any more of right now.

'It isn't just that,' Lara said, pressing a hand to her forehead and trying to think rationally. Already there was a musty smell drifting from the soaked wood floor and bubbling wallpaper. 'It stinks in here—it'll permeate my stock. I'm hardly going to dominate the market with seductive lingerie that smells like a damp garden shed, am I? Not exactly alluring and sensuous, is it? And even if I could leave it here, there'll be workmen traipsing through. I can't risk any further damage. My back's against the wall with the shop opening next week. And I can't stay here anyway if there's no running water.'

She could hear the upset nasal tone in her own voice and bit down hard on her lip to suppress it. She didn't do emotional outbursts. That kind of thing elicited sympathy and she was far too self-reliant to want or need any of that. But she'd given her everything to this shop project and now it felt as if all her hard work had hit standstill in the space of ten minutes.

Poppy, who clearly didn't know or care about the not-liking-sympathy thing, joined her on the sofa, put an arm around her shoulders and gave her an encouraging smile and a squeeze.

'Come and stay with us for a few days, then, until it's sorted out,' she said. 'The boxroom's free—you'd be welcome to it. It's pretty titchy, but at least it's dry. And even better...' she waited until Lara looked at her and threw her hands up triumphantly '...I have running water! Cheer up, it'll all seem better when your hair doesn't look like a ferret's nest.'

Lara felt her lip twitch.

Poppy's grin was warm and friendly. But still the shake of the head came automatically to her, like a tic or an ingrained stock reaction. Lara Connor didn't take help or charity. She'd got where she was relying only on herself.

'I couldn't possibly impose on you like that,' she said. 'I'll be perfectly fine. I'll figure something out myself.'

Figuring something out herself had featured in a big way on her path in life. Taking offers of help didn't come easily to Lara. Relying on other people was a sure-fire route to finding yourself let down.

'You've got a headful of shampoo and no running water,' Poppy pointed out.

Lara touched her hair lightly with one hand. It was beginning to itch now, and seemed to be drying to a hideous crispy cotton-wool kind of texture. She hesitated. Her back really was against the wall over the shop. She groped for some kind of alternative solution that she could handle on her own but none presented itself. Even if she had enough room at the pop-up shop to store all her extra stock, she couldn't exactly move in and live there, could she? There was one tiny back room with a toilet, no furniture, no space, no chance.

'Stop being ridiculous,' Poppy said in a case-closed tone of voice. 'It really is *not* such a big deal. It makes perfect sense. I've got a spare room and you're stuck for a day or two. Where's the problem?'

'I don't like to impose,' Lara evaded.

Poppy made a dismissive chuffing noise.

'If you were imposing, I wouldn't ask you,' she said. 'Come on, it'll be a laugh. Things have been a bit quiet since Izzy moved in with Harry—it'll be nice to have someone else around for a bit.' She stood up. 'You can get straight in the shower and rinse that shampoo out, and then you can ring your landlord and sort out a plumber.' She made for the door as if the subject was closed.

Poppy made it all sound so straightforward. But then of course she had a proper family background, supportive childhood and, let's not forget, her big brother on the premises. She had no need to let coping with a crisis be complicated by things like pride and self-reliance and managing by yourself.

'Just a couple of days, though,' Lara qualified, finally giving in and following her. 'Just until the water's sorted out, and I'll pay rent, of course.'

With what exactly, she wasn't sure. But she would find a way. She always did. Being indebted to someone really wasn't her.

'It's only small, I know...' Poppy said apologetically.

'It's absolutely perfect,' Lara said, wondering vaguely how she could possibly fit all her stock in here. The room was tiny, the only furnishings a small dresser and lamp and the narrowest single bed Lara had ever seen. But in terms of living space, it was a gift. She supposed it might seem small to Poppy and her friends. Lara had heard them talk about boarding school and their families; spacious living was clearly the norm. Lara had had many bedrooms over the years. The dispensable bedroom was part of the package when you were working your way through the care system. She'd lived with a succession of foster families over the years and a room of your own still felt like something to be prized. And after the flood debacle, it really was. 'I can't thank you enough,' she said. 'All I need to do now is source some storage for the rest of my stock. Until the shop gets going I've got a bit of a stockpile. I'll have a look and see if there's somewhere locally that I can keep it cheaply.'

Poppy flapped a hand at her.

'There's no need for that. You don't want to be putting those gorgeous clothes in some hideous manky lockup. You can keep them in Alex's room—there's tons of space in there.' She led the way along the hall and opened the door on what was possibly the neatest room Lara had ever seen. The bed was made with symmetrical coin-bouncing perfection, the top sheet neatly folded back in a perfect white stripe across the top of the quilt. She narrowed her eyes as she took in the radiator, the ends of which were visible either side of the headboard. Goodness knew what acrobatics he'd been performing in this room to make the hideous racket she'd had to put up with.

After the cosy bohemian colour of the rest of the flat, the room was practically austere. Poppy moved to one side so Lara could see properly. Open shelving ran the length of the opposite wall, filled with perfectly folded rectangles of knitwear and T-shirts. Gleamingly polished shoes were lined up neatly in pairs along the lowest shelf. A shelf was devoted to books, their spines lined up in order of height. Not an item was out of place, not a speck of dust marred the clear floor space. A dark oak wardrobe stood at the side of the window. Lara imagined his shirts and jackets would be hung in colour co-ordinated perfection if she were to look inside.

'Wow,' she breathed.

'I know,' Poppy said, completely unfazed. 'He's a million times more tidy and organised than I am. That's what comes of being packed off to boarding school at the age of five and then later going into the military. He's the most organised, methodical person I know.'

A pang of sympathy twisted in Lara's chest at the thought of Alex as a five-year-old fending for himself when he had a family of his own back at home. She'd been forced into that situation by necessity; there simply hadn't been an alternative for her mother. She couldn't comprehend why anyone would want to send their child away when they didn't have to, and they probably paid a fortune for the privilege too.

'He does all his own washing and ironing,' Poppy was saying. 'He just needs a bit of, well, female influence in his life.'

Lara looked at her with raised eyebrows. Female influence? Poppy grinned at her.

'Maybe not *that* kind of female influence. I'm not sure he's short of that.'

He certainly wasn't, judging by the frequency of his overnight guests.

'He needs someone a bit more long-term in my opinion. He's spent far too long with only blokes for company. Who knows? Perhaps a roomful of lingerie might put him in touch with his feminine side a bit more.'

'Are you sure he won't mind having the clothes rails in here?' Lara said doubtfully. 'I mean, it's so *tidy*. I've got quite a lot of loose stuff too.'

Poppy shrugged.

'I'm doing him a favour here, letting him stay. It's my flat, after all.' She tossed her hair back. 'Do you want a hand moving in?'

CHAPTER THREE

HEADING TOWARDS MIDNIGHT, and the landing and stairs were customarily dark as Alex propelled his latest evening companion towards the top flat—Name: Susie; Age: Twenty-six; Occupation: Medical Secretary; Favourite Drink: Strawberry Daiquiri…whatever the hell that was. He'd need to ask Isaac—although he'd bought a few this evening.

He opened the front door and ushered Susie down the dimly lit hallway to his bedroom. The rest of the flat was quiet. Poppy could sleep for England and Isaac was still out of the country. This last week after his encounter with the quiet freak downstairs, Alex had found himself grudgingly attempting to keep the noise down and so he skipped his usual stop-off in the kitchen for a nightcap. Not that it had anything to do with any personal regard for Lara Connor, of course, although he had to admit to a nod of admiration for her business drive. It was more a desire to keep her off his back and live an easy life. And after the embarrassment of sleeping the day away in her flat, he'd done his best to avoid bumping into her again. To that end, he'd also shifted his bed away from the wall a little. Apparently it had worked, since he hadn't heard a word from her since.

As he opened his bedroom door it was the scent that hit him first. It assaulted him even before he flipped the light switch and it put him immediately on edge. Sweet floral notes that took him right back to the rose garden at his family home in the country. The memory wasn't a particularly welcome one. Then again there were precious few childhood memories that were. Susie hung on to his arm and stifled a tipsy giggle, which trailed away as light flooded the room.

'*This* is your room?' Her voice registered shocked disgust, and the fun tone was completely gone, as if he'd lobbed a jug of cold water over her for perfect instant sobriety. She let go of his arm. 'Oh, my God, you *live with someone*,' she wailed. 'I knew it was too good to be true. Where is she—out somewhere? Working?'

The perfect order by which he'd lived his life since he was just a small kid at boarding school, reinforced first by the cadets and then by the army, had been completely in evidence when he'd left the flat some six hours ago for his usual Friday night out. A place for everything and everything squarely in its place. In his absence the room had been inexplicably turned into what looked like a bordello. Clothes racks full of silk and satin nightwear stood alongside the wall; the floor space to one side of the room was stacked with baskets of frilly knickers and lacy bras; there was an overflowing box full of bars of ladies' French soap from which the cloying girly smell was emanating and, most unbelievably, there was a padded clothes hanger over the door of his wardrobe on which hung a long and flowing peacock-blue silk dressing-gown thing trimmed with matching marabou feathers. He felt as if he'd stumbled into some insane dream world.

He suddenly remembered Susie standing next to him and shook his head lightly as if to clear it.

'I'm not with anyone,' he said. 'I'm single.'

Her tone now shifted to sickened.

'You mean this stuff is *yours*? I should have listened to my friends, all those warnings about one-night stands and weirdos. Where's my phone?' She opened her handbag and began to paw through it. 'What are you, some kind of cross-dresser?'

'Of course not,' he said, exasperated. 'For Pete's sake, do I *look* like I might enjoy wearing women's clothing?'

'They never do,' she said, pulling out her phone and scrolling through it. 'I've watched enough reality TV to know that the ones to watch out for are the masculine types. And they never choose the kind of clothes that blend in either, oh, no. It's always a bloody prom dress.' She pointed an emphatic finger at him. 'Or a silk negligee.'

The situation was careering way out of control. He held up placating hands.

'There's obviously been some kind of a mix-up,' he said.

'Too right there has.' She turned away from him. 'Taxi, please,' she snapped into the phone. 'I'll be waiting outside Ignite, Lancaster Road, Notting Hill.'

'It's probably something to do with my sister,' he called after her as she marched back down the hallway to the front door.

'Yeah, yeah. I bet that's what they all say!' she yelled back over her shoulder.

He heard her high-heeled shoes clattering down the stairs as she made a swift exit. He turned back to his room, took in the clutter of girly clothing and breathed in the head-reeling scent of roses.

He'd had enough trouble sleeping when the room was the epitome of calm and orderliness. How the hell was he meant to manage now?

Lara woke to the muffled banging of knuckles on a door and floundered for a moment to get her bearings in the dark. She felt vaguely closed in.

It came slowly back to her overtired brain.

Flooded studio. Damaged stock. Poppy's boxroom.

The knocking continued and she wondered vaguely if it was the front door. Sex-god Alex must have locked himself out again. There was a hint of self-righteous satisfaction in that thought, especially after what she'd learned this afternoon from the emergency plumber who'd investigated the root cause of her flooded flat. A ten-minute conversation had made it clear the flood problem went a lot deeper than a need for a new washer. The old fire station might have had a modern makeover when it was converted to flats but it turned out the glossy living space papered over some serious cracks in the original pipe network. It all made perfect sense now. The pipes servicing her flat were clearly linked to those above and below, hence the insane racket from Alex's bedroom activities travelling down so effectively to her bedroom underneath.

In fact, according to the plumber, the pipework showed signs of recent stress—clearly this was what had caused the plumbing to give up the ghost. So not only was her lack of sleep down to Poppy's sex-crazed brother, but now the flooding of her flat could be attributed to him too. He was fast becoming her least favourite person and therefore any initial guilt she might have felt about imposing on him by using his bedroom to store her stuff had been very easily suppressed.

The brief temptation to just let him knock all night was trumped by the desire to tell him exactly what she thought of his nocturnal activities, the damage of which had now surpassed simple noise pollution. She threw the covers back and grabbed her robe from the back of the door.

Turned out the knocking was coming from inside the flat. She'd been right about one thing though: it was Alex again.

'Is no disruption too inconsiderate for you?' she snapped. He jumped and turned to look at her. She had a mad sense of déjà vu at the sight of him with upraised knuckles hammering on Poppy's bedroom door. Except that this time he was fully dressed. The dark blue shirt made his eyes look almost slate in the dim hallway light and her stomach gave an unexpected flip.

The ability to speak momentarily disappeared because it felt as if his tongue was stuck to the roof of his mouth. Lara's soft blond hair lay in messy bed-head waves over her shoulders. She wore a pink silk dressing gown, with wide sleeves, that ended a good couple of inches above her knees. His eyes dipped to her legs before he could stop them. The slight sheen of the silk against her skin seemed to give it a porcelain quality and the pink colour of the gown picked out the soft fullness of her mouth. He floundered for speech as the unexplained transformation of his bedroom made sudden sense. Was she somehow *staying* here? Why the hell would she be doing that when she had her own perfectly good bedroom down one flight of stairs?

The door clicked open behind him and Poppy finally staggered out, yawning and squinting at the light.

'What the hell's all the noise about? I'm on duty in a few hours.'

He took his eyes off Lara, not without some difficulty, and rounded on his sister. She looked at him with one half-lidded eye.

'My bedroom looks like a tart's boudoir,' he snapped. 'What the hell is going on?'

'For Pete's sake, it's just a few pairs of knickers,' she protested, an incredulous tone to her voice as if his room didn't look like some vintage cathouse. 'There's been a flood in Lara's flat so I've invited her to stay in the boxroom. She needed to store some of her stock for a bit and since there's *masses* of spare space in your bedroom, I couldn't see the problem. Can't this wait until the morning?'

'No, it can't,' he snapped back. 'Have you seen it in there? You didn't even ask me. It's an invasion of my privacy and I'm not going to stand for it.'

He'd always known Poppy's patience was not at its best when she was tired and he braced himself for a sibling argument of monumental proportions.

She drew herself up to her full height.

'Don't, then. Find yourself another flat if you don't like it. Or you could go back home.'

A low blow, and he could tell by the way she shifted her eyes away from him that she knew it. The subject of their inheritance from their grandparents hung between them as strongly as if it had been a visible sack of cash in the corner of the hallway. After getting access to it at the age of twenty-one, Poppy had put hers away, stashed it sensibly for the future, and now she had this flat to show for it. Living for the moment, he'd frittered his away on swanky nights out with Isaac while at university and later while on leave from the army. Expensive holidays were the order of the day. When he had time to himself, he made that time count. One particular ill-judged week in Las Vegas with the lads had reduced the pot considerably. He hadn't given it a thought at the time, hadn't needed to, because he'd had a *career*. Now that career was cut short he found he didn't have the funds any longer for a house deposit, and he needed what was left to start over. Without Poppy's offer of a place to stay he really would be reduced to returning to the family home and the thought filled him with distaste. If it was a choice between that and living in a room full of knickers, he'd just have to put up.

Poppy cast exasperated hands up at the ceiling when he didn't respond.

'I can't *do* this. I am *not* discussing your sleeping arrangements at one in the morning when I've got to be at work in a few hours. The underwear stays. You either put up with it or you move out.' She turned away and stopped any further argument by shutting her bedroom door on him. He stared at the panelled wood, feeling Lara's eyes on his back.

'She loves me really,' he said.

'I'll be out of your hair as soon as the plumbing's fixed in my flat,' Lara said, and instead of what should surely be an apologetic tone he picked up an undeniable pointed edge to her voice.

'Plumbing?'

She leaned against the hallway wall and crossed her arms. His mind insisted on noticing how the silk of the gown lovingly clung to her perfect curves. By act of sheer will, he kept his eyes on her face.

'Yes, plumbing,' she said. 'Turns out your energetic nocturnal activities have put the pipe network under too much strain.'

He stared at her.

'What the hell are you talking about?'

'Half the plumbing in this place is years old—it dates back way before the flat conversion. They might have built things to last back then, but no one reckoned on your bed being shoved up against it. The pipe running down from your bedroom radiator finally gave up the ghost today. It dislodged and because my flat's directly below it caused a flood. I've got no running water down there and damaged stock, and if it wasn't for Poppy I haven't a clue what I'd do.'

'I moved the bed away from the radiator,' he protested.

'Too little too late,' she said, and as she spoke he noticed the dark smudges beneath the indignant eyes. A twist of guilt spiked in his stomach because he'd seen how completely immersed she was in her damned pop-up-shop project. In terms of actually living a productive life right now, he'd just slipped into negative territory. Living a quiet life and not hacking anyone off surely wasn't meant to be this hard. The feeling of uselessness and lack of direction that he'd been shoving away pretty much since he'd returned to London made a sudden gut-churning comeback.

She looked on as he passed a hand tiredly over his forehead. She could feel the climb down as he spread his hands.

'Look, I'm sorry about the flood. You're sure it was down to me?'

An apology? And a marginally more genuine one this time since he really didn't have anything to gain from it. He wasn't shut out on the landing half naked now, was he? In acknowledgement she curbed her angry tone a little.

'According to the emergency plumber, the problem originated in the area of pipework attached to your radiator, so that would be a yes.'

He made a move towards the kitchen and she followed him and watched from the doorway as he filled the kettle.

'Hot drink?' he said, eyebrows raised.

She shook her head and he took a single mug from the drainer.

'Any idea on timescale?' he said. 'How long do I have to live in a *frou-frou* bordello?'

'Do you mind? My stuff is classy, not tarty,' she snapped.

He sighed. 'Of course it is.'

'The plumber did that thing where they suck in their breath and shake their head pityingly,' she said. 'I'm guessing at least a few days. Plus you have to factor in the weekend. He's made it safe but he's not going to actually *do* much else until Monday.'

He thrust an enormous heaped spoonful of instant coffee into the mug and topped it up with hot water.

'You're really going to drink that now?' she said, eyeing it. 'You'll be buzzing.'

He glanced at her. She could see the dark circles beneath his eyes even from here. Why would anyone who looked that tired want a caffeine boost?

'Yup.'

He turned around to face her, leaning back against the worktop. Her heart rate upped its pace a notch at the intense look in the grey eyes. The last time she'd been this close to him he'd been asleep, his face relaxed. Now he looked drawn and tense. He looked as if he needed a good night's sleep.

'You mentioned some stock was damaged,' he said.

She nodded and sighed.

'Some camisoles,' she said and, seeing his questioning frown, added, 'like vest tops, you know, with the string-type shoulder straps. Also some silk knickers.'

There was no denying it had been a setback. The water marks had ruined them.

He shifted awkwardly on his feet, clearly not massively comfortable with discussing women's underwear in the early hours of the morning.

'Look, I know I can't make up for the time you've lost but at least let me pay for the damage,' he said, his hand sliding around to the back pocket of his jeans. He produced a wallet and opened it.

She looked at him, surprised. An apology *and* an offer to make amends.

'It's fine,' she said, shaking her head. 'It's enough that Poppy's letting me stay here. That's a massive help. I hadn't a clue what I was going to do.'

'That doesn't help with your stock damage, though, does it?' Completely ignoring her, he pulled a wad of notes free. She stared at them, a hundred different things running through her mind that she could do if she had an extra cash injection. She rejected them all.

How easy it must be to just have access to that kind of money whenever you needed it, just paying off your problems when they arose. He probably had a massive trust fund at his disposal. She might have her back against the wall and no ready cash but what she had to show for it had never been handed to her on a plate. Everything she had was the result of hard graft. That was the way she wanted it. She didn't want to feel beholden to any-one else, that way she knew any success was hers alone and couldn't be snatched away. Yes, the pipes breaking might have been down to Alex but the whole pipe system was shot to hell as it was and there was no way she would be accepting his money. She would never have taken up Poppy's offer if she hadn't been desperate.

'I don't want your money,' she said, holding a hand up to stop his outstretched handful of notes.

He hesitated a moment, watching her face intently, and then put the money away.

'OK, then.' He took a sip of the coffee that was so black it looked like engine oil. 'But if there's anything I can do to help, let me know.'

Throwaway comment or genuine offer, she didn't know. At least he'd accepted responsibility. Her opinion of him stepped up the tiniest notch.

'I will,' she said, knowing she wouldn't. She turned for the door and headed back to bed, leaving him to sip his horrible drink and wondering what the hell problem he had with normal sleep patterns.

Sleeping in the daytime had a major drawback, Alex now found. Pitch darkness was almost impossible to achieve, background noise kept rousing him, and every time he came awake he was faced with the hideous violation of his ordered personal space. Staring at the four walls of his room in Poppy's flat was a great deal less palatable and restful now that they were festooned with women's underwear.

He eventually gave up at around three in the afternoon, showered, dressed and headed out for a head-clearing walk. The October Saturday afternoon was crisp and sunny as he turned onto Portobello Road with its buzz of shoppers. The colour and pace was rousing. He was almost past the shop before he realised it was Lara's, his overtired brain only processing the eye-catching pink and black sign when he'd taken half a dozen paces onwards.

He stopped in his tracks and backed up, looking up above the gleaming glass window, to where 'Boudoir Fashionista' was painted in a curly black handwritten font on a pink background. Another sign hung on the closed door. 'Opening Soon', it said.

Not that he hadn't had his absolute *fill* of frilly underwear back in his own home, but curiosity nonetheless meant he couldn't stop himself from just having a quick look to see what her big dream of a pop-up shop looked like inside. He moved to the glass and framed his hands around his eyes to see in.

Inside, with just a couple of overhead lights on, he could make out a counter at the back of the small shop floor, open shelving that was currently empty, some stacks of boxes, and, in the middle of it all, Lara, apparently trying to heft a package that was at least twice as big as she was across the floor. It teetered on one corner and looked momentarily as if it might topple through the plate-glass window taking her with it. What the hell was she thinking?

Before he knew what he was doing he was trying the door, and when it didn't open he knocked on it, hard. He watched as she heaved the package to lean against the wall and then practically saw her eyes roll as she clocked him watching her. She crossed to the door, undid a few bolts and opened it.

'What are you doing here?' she said. She certainly didn't sound pleased to see him.

'One wrong move and you'll be pinned under that thing for a week,' he said 'What the hell are you doing humping furniture like that around on your own?'

She glanced across at the six-foot-high package of tape and bubble wrap.

'It's a full-length mirror. I'm trying to decide where I want it.' She tilted her chin up indignantly. 'And I'm not an invalid. I'm perfectly capable of moving a few sticks of furniture around.'

Sticks of furniture? The mirror was enormous, a good couple of feet taller than she was and generously wide.

'Don't be ridiculous, you'll end up in traction. And then where will your damn pop-up shop be?' He walked straight past her into the shop and crossed to the packaged mirror. 'Where do you want it?'

For the umpteenth time he rested the mirror against the wall of the shop and watched as Lara leaned back and surveyed the floor as a whole. The shop door was closed again, but through the plate-glass window he could see shoppers rubbernecking in interest at them. She'd painted the walls the palest of rose pink. The floor was polished wood and there was an original fireplace to one side. Lara had made the most of the feature, stringing it with pale pink silk flowers and white pin lights. In the centre of the small floor space there was now a low oval French-style table painted cream. The small counter at the back of the shop had a tongue-and-groove effect in cream-painted wood and there was a painted wooden dressing screen with scrolled edging that Lara kept moving around because she couldn't decide where she wanted the chang-

ing-room area to be. The whole effect was girly enough
to have him feeling completely out of his comfort zone.

'What about there?' he asked, without much hope.
She'd had him move the damn thing all over the place,
trying out all four walls and every corner.

She shook her head, one finger tapping at the side of
her chin.

'No, I think I liked it best the way we had it first.'

He squashed his exasperation, not without some difficulty. He could appreciate perfectionism as much as
the next military man but this…

He caught her looking at him, an apologetic smile
playing at the corner of the lush mouth.

'I'm sorry. I'm a nightmare, I know. I just want so
much for it to be perfect.'

'No problem.'

He moved the mirror back to where it had started nearly
an hour ago. In the interim she'd got on with decorating the
shop around him, stopping every now and then to order
him about. There was a part of him that couldn't fail to be
impressed by her drive and determination. Not to mention
the fact that her dreams were mapped out. She had a game
plan that she was clearly taking in stages. And no wonder
he was intrigued by that in light of the fact that his life was
currently cruising along with absolutely zero direction.

'So what's the big deal about refusing help?' he said,
glancing at her as she watched him heft the mirror
around. 'I mean, I did *offer* the other night. You could
have just spoken up then that you needed some fittings
moving around.'

'I didn't want to impose. I'm doing enough of that just
by staying at the flat.'

He shrugged.

'It's no big deal. Poppy wouldn't have offered if it was. She'd do the same for any of her friends.'

His blasé tone made it clear he thought she was making a mountain out of nothing. Of course he would think that. The rich were surrounded by freeloaders, weren't they? Hangers-on probably came with the territory, and she couldn't bear the thought of being seen like that.

'I guess I'm just used to doing things by myself, that's all,' she said. 'Problems come up, I find my own way round them. I don't like to take anything or anyone for granted, so I get things done myself.'

She'd made that mistake far too often when she was a kid to make it again now.

'Even if it means getting trapped under something heavy?' he said. 'You can't shift furniture like this about yourself,' he added, his tone appalled. 'You really will injure yourself.'

'Of course I can,' she said indignantly. 'I put up the shelves myself. I painted the walls myself. I can hump and bump a bit of furniture around.'

Not that it hadn't been too heavy for her. He was right about that: it had been a struggle. Whereas he could clearly shift furniture around all day without breaking a sweat.

'Yeah, well,' he said gruffly. 'Any more of that needs doing and I want you to ask me.'

She opened her mouth to politely decline the offer and he held up a hand to stop her.

'As a favour,' he said. 'For Pete's sake, accept some help. I'm not asking you to sign your name in blood.'

His tone was final, subject closed and she found herself inclining her head in acknowledgement, not that she

would stick at it if the situation arose. She couldn't deny
it was nice to have the fittings finished in here and it
would have taken her twice as long on her own, but she
certainly didn't intend to make a habit of leaning on anyone else. Especially him.

'You're very driven,' he said, changing the subject.

She crossed to the wooden counter and pulled herself
up so she was sitting on it.

'Yeah, well, it's been a dream for a long time. Finally
trialling a shop is a really big deal for me. There's a lot
riding on it.'

Her entire savings just for starters.

'How did you get into it?' he said. 'I mean, isn't it a
pretty niche market, underwear?'

His tone was vaguely awkward and a smile rose on her
lips at his obvious fish-out-of-waterness when it came
to discussing lingerie. She imagined he would be the
type of man she sometimes encountered on her market
stall, obviously out of their depth as they chose underwear for a wife or girlfriend with no clue about bra size
or colour choice.

'I've always been into sewing,' she said. 'It's grown
from that really. Specialising in lingerie came later when
I went to college. I'm inspired by vintage fashion, that
Hollywood era where women were glossy, curvy, glamorous. When I designed my first collection I based my
ideas on that.'

She watched him positioning the mirror, not looking
at her, and her mind drifted back down the years. She
hadn't been into much of anything really as a child, apart
from keeping her head down. Until she'd been fostered by
Bridget, that was. The last in a long line of foster homes

where Lara had apparently not been a good fit. Being a *good fit* was a hideously elusive thing. She'd tried everything over the years to be that. Living with Bridget was the one and only time she'd come even close. She'd ended up staying there until she was old enough to go to college. Bridget had been a seamstress and had taught Lara everything she knew. And finding something she was not only good at but was also passionate about had been the biggest turning point in her life.

She'd realised while at college that she was talented at dressmaking. On the heels of that came the realisation that she could make a living at this if she wanted to. She could make her own stability, her own home life, without having to rely on anyone else. If she worked hard enough she'd never need to worry about being a good fit ever again. She'd have a life of her own.

'You decided against working for anyone else?' he said.

She shrugged.

'I started out that way, did some time for a high-street fashion line. But I'm a bit of a control freak. I like doing things my way. I like the idea of making my own success. I know I can rely on myself, you see. I won't be letting myself down.'

'And you learned to sew before college?'

The mirror was in place. He took a step back.

'That's perfect,' she said, jumping down from the counter. She crossed the shop to join him and began tugging the polystyrene corners and protective film off the mirror, revealing a gilt scrolled frame and flawless glass. He moved in to help her. 'I learned to sew when I was about fourteen.'

'Your mum taught you?'

She looked at him for a moment. He'd shifted a bit of furniture around. Was she really going to kid herself that he wanted to hear her life story? He was probably just being polite, filling the silences.

'Something like that,' she said.

She bundled the packaging up into a ball and shoved it into the corner next to a couple of bin bags, then turned back to survey her shop floor. It was exactly as she wanted it and excitement sparkled through her at how the project was coming together. Before she could stop herself she'd reached out to touch his arm. He looked down at her hand in surprise.

'Thanks for helping out,' she said. 'I owe you a favour.'

For the first time since she'd met him, she got a smile that didn't have an undertone of exasperation about it. It creased his grey eyes at the corner and lifted the strong mouth. He really was gorgeous and her stomach gave an unexpected flutter.

'I'll think of something,' he said.

CHAPTER FOUR

ALEX THREW HIMSELF bolt upright, panic racing through his veins, certain he'd just shouted out loud.

It had been the same as always. The windows bursting into cracks, held in place by their film covering. The feeling and sound of massive pressure beneath the vehicle as the explosion ripped through it. Smoke and dust filling the space around him, the air thick with it. He could taste the explosives in his mouth. Then the aftermath, the melting hot asphalt on the road beneath him and the disorientation as he staggered through smoke and wreckage to look for Sam and for the driver of the vehicle. Private Sam Walker had been accompanying him. One of his unit, one of his own.

He stared around him in panic, a twist of sheet clutched in one fist and the pillows damp against his back.

There was a book open to one side of the bed where he'd been trying to stave off sleep by reading. Late autumn's golden sunlight slanted through the gap in the curtains. And the bedroom was full of ladies' underwear.

His pulse slowly began to climb down towards normal, his breathing began to level. Somehow the festooning of his room with lingerie and nightwear put such a mad skew on his surroundings that it calmed him in a way

his usual military-ordered bedroom didn't. This was reality. There was no way of confusing this room with his
army existence. He was home. He was no longer part of
the army. His responsibility was discharged.

He checked his watch. Late morning. He must have finally dropped off to sleep around five. It could be worse.
Six hours' uninterrupted sleep wasn't a bad count by
recent standards. And he couldn't have shouted aloud.
Poppy and Lara were probably hanging around the flat;
they would have heard, Poppy would have burst in here
without a moment's thought. He swung his feet off the
bed and headed for the shower, stood under the torrent of
hot water. Maybe this was what counted for an improvement; maybe he would be able to get longer and longer
stretches of sleep until he could find some level of normality. He would not succumb to these nightmares. He
would get through this.

Strong coffee. That was what he needed now to get rid
of the last grasping tendrils of the dream. Five minutes
later and he was heading downstairs to the ground-floor
café and its industrial-strength espresso.

Ignite channelled quirky but cosy with a nod to the history of the building from the original fireman's pole still
in the middle of the shop. Framed black and white wall
prints hung on the exposed brickwork of the walls, show-
ing the building when it was a fire station instead of a
block of flats. It ran a steady trade in Sunday brunch, the
air was filled with the delicious smell of frying bacon and
hot coffee and Lara was sitting at the corner table with a
pot of tea, a laptop and an untouched blueberry muffin.

She didn't even glance up as he walked in, and he
watched her at his leisure as he waited to pay for his

coffee. Her blond hair was piled up on her head today, a pink fabric flower pinned at one side, and she was wearing a fitted floral blouse that showed off her curves to perfection. In terms of distraction she easily beat Marco, who stood behind the counter, and a surge of heated interest spiked through him—interest that hadn't really come to the fore when he'd had her pegged as annoying neighbour. There was no need to fudge the fact he was looking at her because her entire attention was focused on the open laptop screen. Did she never do downtime?

'It's Sunday,' he said, coming to a standstill, coffee in hand, next to her table.

She looked up at him, china-blue eyes wide.

'And your point?'

'You're working,' he said. 'Again. Do you never take a break?'

'I *am* taking a break,' she protested. 'I'm updating my blog and I'm checking over my launch fliers and thinking about where I can hand them out.' She pushed the opposite chair out with one of her ballet flats. 'Sit down—you can tell me what you think.'

'Not sure I like what it says about me, that you think my opinion on women's lingerie might have value,' he said. Then the immediate need for coffee won over and he sat down and took the pale pink piece of stiff card she held out.

'You'd be surprised how many of my customers are men,' she said. 'Hanging round the market stall looking awkward, usually on a quest for something red with peepholes. I soon put them straight. Women like classy and glamorous, not tarty.' She pointed at him with her pen. 'So, actually, I'd be interested in your feedback.'

He looked over the invitation with its loopy black handwriting and silhouette image of a curvy female form.

'You're having a launch party on Thursday night?' he said.

She nodded.

'I'm opening from six until eight. Late-night shopping with pink champagne and nibbles, that kind of thing. You'll come, won't you?' She swept on breezily before he could get in an immediate thanks-but-no-thanks. 'I've invited half the building to drop by. Poppy's coming, and Izzy and Tori. I just need to drum up as much interest as I can, need to think about where I can hand these out. Marco says I can put a stack of them on the counter in here.' She pressed a hand to her forehead. 'And I'm doing a big post about it on my blog, and then I need to keep building up the anticipation on the Facebook page. Not to mention tweeting about it…'

He held up a hand to stop the stream-of-consciousness torrent.

'You'll drive yourself into an early grave. When did you last take a break?'

She waved a hand at the untouched blueberry muffin and half-full teacup and raised her eyebrows.

'This is *not* a break,' he said, exasperated. 'You're putting yourself under far too much pressure. What you need is fresh air and exercise.' The words were out of his mouth before he registered what he was doing. 'Come for a run with me this afternoon.'

She stared at him as if he'd just suggested she jog naked down Portobello Road.

'Are you insane? I don't do running.'

'I know,' he said. 'I can tell by the way you're so manic. Physical fitness feeds the mind. You'll be able to work twice as efficiently afterwards.' He nodded at her muffin. 'Much better than the sugar rush you'll get from eating that stodge.'

She narrowed her eyes at him, as if trying to decide whether he was joking.

'Really?'

He nodded, taking a huge swig of his coffee.

'One hour. You can spare one hour. And you do owe me a favour. I'm fed up with running on my own.'

It was becoming clear that being alone with his thoughts might not be the best therapy for dwelling on the past. And testing though it might have been heaving furniture around her shop the previous day, it had also been the first hour in a while that he'd been engaged enough by something that the past hadn't encroached on his thoughts. The rest of the day yawned emptily ahead of him without his current distraction of choice—female company. And it occurred to him as she leaned forward to speak to him, giving him a fabulous view of her perfect creamy cleavage, that he was a fool. There was no sense in trawling bars and clubs on Sunday daytime when he had a perfectly good contender right here.

'I meant cooking you lunch or buying you a coffee,' she said. 'Not letting you distract me from my work to run round Notting Hill like a headless chicken.'

'My runs are structured, not some random dash,' he countered. 'You're so manic that you'll probably find it calming to do something physical for a change.'

She paused.

'And we can distribute some leaflets while we're out,' he said.

She tilted her chin upwards in a way that told him *that* was the real pull for her in this scenario. Everything she did seemed to be about furthering her damn business plan.

'Done,' she said. 'And I am *not* bloody manic.'

She slammed the downstairs door of the flats behind her and saw that he was already there. Ready and waiting for her in running gear that was worn in enough to show he took his fitness extremely seriously. She glanced longingly through the window of Ignite, where she could be sitting right now with her laptop and a doughnut. She forced a smile, turned to face him and clocked his bemused expression.

'What?' she said as he looked her up and down. 'I'm not some gym bunny, you know, with all the kit. I did the best I could in the time.' She looked down at herself. 'I borrowed the running shoes and shorts from Poppy. The T-shirt's my own. I embellished it myself.'

'You don't say,' Alex said, staring at the loose cotton T-shirt, the front of which was smothered in a sprinkling of pink sequins. Her hair was caught up in a ponytail and tied with a pink scarf and she was wearing pink lipstick. He wondered for a moment why the hell he had thought this would be a good idea.

She moved behind him and unzipped his backpack.

'What the hell are you doing now?'

A wave of her floral perfume as she leaned in close to him knocked his senses off-kilter. He craned around to see her stuff a wad of her pink leaflets into the bag.

'This is meant to be for an energy drink, or an iPod, or a mobile phone, not masses of stuff,' he grumbled.

'It's just a few leaflets,' she said, totally ignoring him and zipping it back up. 'No need to roll your eyes—you must be used to lugging ten-stone backpacks across deserts for days at a time. A few slips of paper are hardly going to weigh you down.'

He nodded down the street.

'Holland Park's in that direction. Brisk walk first,' he said as she began limbering up and jogging from foot to foot. 'You need to warm up properly, don't want to pull any muscles.'

She kept pace with him as he started down the road, and five minutes later they turned into the park. Holland Park was quiet and peaceful with lots of open green space, but also nature trails and walkways and a stunning Japanese garden. The ground was covered in temptingly kickable autumn leaves in red and gold and the air was crisp and clear. Trees filtered golden sunshine. The appeal of running, which had so far eluded her, kicked in. This place was a real haven from the buzz of the city.

There was something about his hugely muscled frame in its well-worn sportswear that made walking fast look cool as opposed to looking as if he were late for a bus or rushing for a toilet. She really wasn't sure she could pull cool off in Poppy's shorts, which were really on the small side for her curvy hips but gaped massively at her waist. She retied the drawstring grimly and tugged her T-shirt down as far as she could.

She must have been mad to agree to this. She could have been spending this time drafting the next couple of days' worth of Facebook posts, uploading the photos she'd taken of some of the new raspberry silk knickers she'd designed with the frills on the butt.

Alex made a valiant effort not to let his eyes slide continually down to her bare legs. This close it was impossible not to notice the smooth cream of her thighs, and there was a fragility to the porcelain skin and blond hair, blue eyes colouring that belied how strong-willed and driven she really was.

'Have you done any running before?' he asked.

She shrugged.

'I've been able to do it since I was a toddler.' She sighed as he pulled an unimpressed face. 'No, I haven't. Not proper running. Not since I was at school. I'm not some madly fit exercise freak—it has to fit around everything else in my life.'

'Any exercise at all?'

'I like swimming,' she said unexpectedly. 'I used to go a lot. No time for it since I came here though. I let everything slide really that isn't related to the business. It's only a couple of months. I wanted to throw everything I've got into it.'

A spike of envy at her sense of purpose jabbed him behind the ribs. He couldn't help admiring her focus and determination, that refusal to let anything divert her from her goal.

'We'll take it steady, then,' he said. 'One minute gentle jogging, then one minute walking. Ready?'

He broke into a slow jog and she followed suit next to him.

'What about relationships?' he said after a moment.

Just because he'd never seen her with a man, didn't mean there wasn't one.

She let out an amused noise alongside her speedy breathing.

'Some of us just don't have time for that stuff,' she panted.

He couldn't fail to miss the barb in that comment.

'Meaning that I do—right?' he said.

He glanced at his watch and slowed down into a walking session, keeping it brisk to maintain the heart rate. She kept pace next to him, clearly not as unfit as she'd made herself sound. Then again, he couldn't remember the last time he'd met anyone with so much energy. She was constantly on the go.

She took the bottle of water he passed to her and took a sip. He was aware of her watching him over the bottle.

'I suppose everyone's entitled to *some* time out,' she conceded. 'How long will you be staying with Poppy? She said something about an honourable discharge. Is that permanent? No going back to the army?' She handed the bottle back.

He gritted his teeth.

'I won't be going back. The discharge is an end to it. That chapter of my life is well and truly over.'

Saying it out loud made it no more palatable. It still felt vaguely unreal, even months later, with everything tied up.

'You don't sound so pleased about that.'

He shrugged.

'I'm not. I didn't want to be discharged—the army was my life.'

She didn't comment for a minute or two, but he could feel her eyes on him.

'I saw your scars,' she said at last. 'When you fell asleep in my flat.' Her voice was full of sympathy. 'I'm really sorry.'

He carried on walking in silence for a moment, noticing she didn't push for any more details. The gap sat there in the conversation, and she was leaving it to him to elaborate.

'There was an incident,' he said eventually. That word seemed so inadequate as a description. The relentless guilt churned sickly in his stomach as he recalled it. Guilt that he was walking through this glorious park while Sam, who he'd promised to look out for, had been gone in an instant on Alex's watch.

'A roadside bomb,' he clarified.

He indicated the left side of his chest lightly. 'This was down to shrapnel—it sliced below my shoulder blade and then settled in my chest muscle. The medics removed it but there wasn't much they could do about the scarring.'

The physical side of the injuries he could talk about. She certainly wasn't the first woman to ask about them. Coping with them and recovering at breakneck speed had been his way of proving his strength, to himself as much as anyone. He clenched his fists lightly. If only putting the experience out of his mind could be as straightforward. Nagging doubt about his mental strength continued to plague him. The sickening guilt that he'd failed Sam was never far away, seething beneath the surface of his mind. He had offered encouragement to that young soldier when he'd struggled at first with his posting. He had helped him get a handle on his fears. He had assured Sam he would look out for him and he'd let him down on an epic scale.

The frustration that he couldn't seem to just fast-track the recovery of his mind in the same way as his body was relentless, and worse was what that said about his strength or weakness as a soldier.

'You're lucky to have your family to support you through something like that,' she said.

The ludicrousness of that comment brought a laugh that he failed to suppress.

'Did I say something funny?'

He glanced sideways at her, saw her puzzled frown and shook his head.

'I'm not laughing at you. My family aren't really like that, except for Poppy. We're not close. Stiff upper lip and all that.'

He kept walking, wondering if she'd let the subject drop now.

'What are your plans now, then?' she said. 'If the army's out of the question.'

Apparently not. He shook his head.

'I haven't got a clue. I've known exactly how my life would play out since I was knee high. There was a long line of military family members to live up to when I was growing up, never any question that was the route I'd take. Tons of army anecdotes bandied around at family gatherings. I enrolled at Sandhurst when I finished university and then pushed myself up the ranks. My future was mapped out. To suddenly not have one is a bit of a curved ball, to be honest.'

Understatement of the year.

'OK, then, well, what was your Plan B? You have to have a back-up plan. Like me, for example, if this pop-up shop doesn't work out then I'll probably look into building up an online presence more, try pushing the internet shopping angle. You must have at least an idea of the direction you want to take, even if you haven't pinned it down to a specific career path.'

'I've never needed a Plan B. What would be the point? My Plan A spanned pretty much the whole of my life. I thought if I took a bit of time out and stayed with Poppy I could work out my next move.' He thought for a moment. 'It would have to be something active, I think. I'm not sure I'm suited to sitting behind a desk.'

She didn't answer and he checked his watch.

'Time's up, let's pick up the pace again,' he said.

Twenty minutes of alternating jogging and brisk walking and he had to admit she wasn't the ditsy glamour girl she seemed. Not entirely anyway. Although he could see from the flush high up on her cheekbones and the damp tendrils of blond hair escaping her ponytail that she'd pushed herself, she'd nonetheless kept pace with him for the full distance.

'You've done well,' he said. 'You sound like you have zero time for exercise but you must be doing something right.'

She shrugged and smiled, pushed a damp lock of hair out of her eyes.

'I'm always on the go. The business keeps me really busy, especially at the moment. I've thrown everything I've got at this pop-up shop. All my spare money's tied up in it. I've got no choice but to make it work.

'Doesn't that worry you, having so much invested in it?'

She smiled.

'If I stopped to worry about everything that could go wrong, I'd never get anywhere. You can't get rid of any risk completely. I mean, I'd planned this move into retail within an inch of its life but I hadn't factored in the problem with the plumbing in my flat. If it hadn't been for Poppy offering me the boxroom I would have been in serious trouble there.' She shrugged. 'But you have to accept some risk if you're going to move forward. Sometimes you just have to put yourself out there to reach your goal.'

It was hard not to get swept along by her drive. That dogged refusal to contemplate failure. She made anything seem possible. Spending time with her was like having an injection of optimism and, goodness knew, he had been in dire need of some of that these past months.

He slowed to a standstill as they approached a fenced-off playground area and nodded at a park bench.

'Need to cool down now,' he said. 'Stretches. Last thing you need is to pull a muscle.'

She followed him reluctantly to the bench and gripped the back of it in the same way he was, self-consciousness kicking back in. A stone's throw away the sandy-floored playground was jam-packed with small children clambering over wooden equipment and rubbernecking Notting Hill mums. Alex Spencer, ex-army, with his honed body hot and sweaty in muscle-hugging sportswear, was clearly a big distraction to the female species at large.

'Now stand on one leg and hold the other leg behind you, hold your foot above the ankle,' he instructed, oblivious to the fluster he was causing in the playground.

Clearly her attempt at the exercise was inadequate because he was suddenly in her personal space, one hand pressed softly at her lower back, holding her steady and the other covering her hand as she gripped her own ankle, holding her foot high behind her. She felt envious eyes boring into her back from the direction of the playground.

'Feel that stretch?' he said.

Maybe she would do, if she weren't too busy feeling unexpectedly *melty* at the closeness of his muscular body and his huge hands on her. There really was no denying how breathtakingly gorgeous he was. There was also no way she was going to have a swooning moment over him. She had far too much on her plate to let *that* kind of distraction slip past her guard.

'Absolutely,' she said loudly.

* * *

Another half-dozen or so stretches out of the way and it occurred to Lara that she was missing a trick right there with Alex's captive audience. Unzipping his small rucksack, she removed a wad of leaflets and crossed to the playground while he leaned against the back of the bench and swigged from a bottle of water.

She walked into the playground and handed a leaflet to anyone who made eye contact.

'Lingerie?' A dark-haired woman with a designer pushchair took a leaflet and read it with interest.

'It's a pop-up shop,' Lara said, full of pride. 'In Portobello Road. Boutique lingerie and nightwear. Vintage inspired. I'm having a launch party on Thursday and I'll be there for the next couple of months. I'd love it if you'd drop in. And tell your friends.'

'Maybe that's the secret, then. I need to get me some boutique lingerie.'

She nodded in Alex's direction with a knowing wink.

Lara laughed out loud, glossing over a deep-down glimmer of pride that it clearly wasn't *that* outrageous a suggestion that she could be the other half of someone who looked like an Adonis.

'We're not together! He's just my...' she searched for the right description '...*running partner.*' As if she had time for daily jogs around parks and sets of stretches. 'Military-style personal training,' she added, purely off the top of her head.

She followed the gaze of the yummy-mummy contingent as Alex, seemingly oblivious to the attention, poured a few lugs of the water over his head and tousled it through his short hair.

The dark-haired woman leaned in towards her.

'Bloody hell, having him as a personal trainer would be way more motivating than the gym.'

'There you go, doesn't your head feel clearer for that?' he said as they headed back to the flat.

Well, she hadn't thought about the shop for half an hour or so, if that was what he meant. Not that it had anything to do with exercise, more about being fascinated by the reality of what she'd simply assumed was a privileged and fabulous upbringing. Plus there was the physical diversion provided simply by looking at him. Of course, she hadn't been the only one seduced by that—he'd had half the playground drooling over him.

'That could be your Plan B, right there,' Lara said, nodding back towards the park as they walked away.

Alex looked sideways at her.

'What do you mean?'

'Personal training,' she said. 'You wouldn't be short of clients. I mean, just look at you. You're a bored lady-who-lunches' dream. You could be the new Zumba.'

'I'm not sure if that's a compliment or an insult,' he said. 'On the whole I'm leaning towards insult.'

'Who cares which it is if you can make money out of it?' she said, her eyes shining. He could almost see her mind ticking over as she thought through whatever insane idea it was she was trying to pitch. 'You could make a killing. Once I'd told them you were just taking me for a run and they got past the fact that we weren't an item I nearly got trampled in the rush. You did *say* you didn't fancy some desk job. You're bored with exercising on your own instead of bawling out squaddies on route marches or whatever, so take on a couple of clients and earn some cash while you're at it. At the very least it could be a stopgap until you decide what you really want to do.'

'I'm not sure,' he said doubtfully, struggling to keep up with the torrential pace of her mind. She totally ignored him.

'OK, then, maybe not *exactly* that, but what I'm saying is you need to put yourself out there, try out some ideas, maybe think outside the box and make your own opportunity. The perfect job isn't just going to materialise like magic and drop in your lap while you hibernate in your sister's flat and pop out every now and then to pull women. What about a fitness boot camp for kids? You've got that military presence thing going on—no one would dare backchat you. The country's full of overweight teenagers sitting playing Call of Duty or chatting on Facebook. You could be a one-man combat for the obesity crisis. I can see it now—*Rid Notting Hill of Couch Potatoes*.' She held her hands up as if imagining the slogan as a headline.

The first spark of positivity he'd had in weeks unexpectedly lifted his spirits. Insane though some of her stream-of-consciousness ideas were, it was hard not to get swept along by her enthusiasm. She made anything seem possible and she was becoming more distracting by the second.

'Oh, and you have to come to the launch now,' she said airily. 'A few of them asked for business cards and, of course, you don't have any, so I handed out my leaflets instead. You could literally *see* their ears prick up when I mentioned you'd be there.'

Oh, just bloody *great*.

As he followed her up the stairs to the flat the rest of the afternoon now seemed to lie empty ahead of him, especially as he was actually feeling positive for a change. Optimistic, even. A half-hour chat with Lara and her energy and enthusiasm was infectious. Already his mind was running with the idea of some kind of business centred around fitness; it could fit his skills set on so many levels.

He didn't want their encounter to be over. It wasn't just that she was so distracting, it was how cute she looked with her blond hair dishevelled for once instead of polished, the flush of her cheeks from the exercise, the smooth shapely legs in the shorts. It was how she made anything seem possible. He liked her. On every level. And since his own fitness level was way above a thirty-minute jog-walk session, he was now a mass of pent-up mental and physical energy. He was at a loose end until the end of the day. Taking all of this into account, the perfect afternoon scenario was obvious.

Prolonging the afternoon with her in his bed would be the perfect solution.

'Would you like to get a drink?' he said, thinking ahead. Drink, chat in the sitting room, ending up in his bedroom.

'Ooh, yes, that would be perfect,' she said. 'Could you make me a pint of lemon squash while I have a quick shower?'

Not exactly what he had in mind. He followed her past the kitchen and she turned back to him at the door of the boxroom, tugging the band out of her hair and ruffling it. Anticipatory sparks were simmering hotly in his stomach at the thought of where this could lead.

'Thanks for the run,' she said. 'I'm expecting my productivity to at least double this afternoon now, otherwise I'll be lodging an official complaint.' She was looking up at him, smile on her face, her eyes shining and cheeks pink from the fresh air and exercise. The relaxed look was such a contrast to her usual polished style and it suited her. She looked absolutely adorable and he reached a hand out to tuck a stray lock of hair behind her ear.

Her initial reaction was shocked surprise at the unexpected touch, and as a result sensibility took a few moments to kick in. A few moments in which he cradled the nape of her neck in one of his huge hands and executed the most deliciously bone-melting kiss she'd ever had. Her body clearly couldn't give a toss about sensibility and kicked straight in with a hike in her heart rate and a mass of hot fluttering in her stomach.

Her mind had been set so resolutely in work mode these last weeks that all thoughts of her personal life had been swept under the carpet. It simply hadn't entered her radar that there could be any more to this than…well, than a *run*. Also, he looked like a sportswear model and she was currently hot, sweaty and wearing a hideous ill-fitting shorts and T-shirt combo. All of which might not have mattered one bit if the fact that he usually picked his women up for one night only hadn't popped into her mind. That last thought brought common sense whizzing back and she disentangled herself from him just as he was sliding his free hand around her waist.

He was clearly at a loose end for the rest of the day and couldn't see the point in going out on the pull when he now had someone living in. Whereas she had three days and counting before the shop launch and a million and one things to do in that short space of time.

She'd had enough disposable people dip in and out of her life to add another one. Relationships in her opinion should be about stability, not about shallow motives, not something that could be picked up and put down on a whim. Not that she hadn't partaken in an occasional flurry of dating, always when she was between projects or had a bit of extra time on her hands, but so far none of those flurries had translated into anything that could survive being shoved aside by what was *really* important in her life: her work ambitions. That held true more than ever right now because things were at such a pivotal point. More than anything she needed to keep focus, keep her wits about her. No being distracted from her goals because she'd been propositioned by the fittest guy she'd come across in years.

She locked her knees before they could slide out from under her.

There was no denying her attraction to him. He could see it in the speed of her breathing and the hard peaks of her nipples through the thin sequinned T-shirt. Nonetheless, deny it she did.

'I'm sorry, Alex.' Just the way she said his name upped the heat in his stomach a notch. 'I've got too much to do to while away an afternoon in bed with you.'

'I wasn't thinking about being idle.'

He saw the blush that comment invoked and liked it.

'And attractive though a hot fling might be to some people, I'm not that kind of girl. And even if I was, I'm juggling enough things as it is right now. I daren't add sex to the mix or the whole lot could go tits up.'

He shrugged.

'There's no need for it to be complicated,' he said. The worst thing he could have said, apparently, because she took an extra pace back and gave him a my-mind-is-made-up smile.

'Why does that not surprise me?' she said. 'I know your routine better than you do. I've lived downstairs from it for weeks. I'm not interested in being one of your disposable pickups, making the walk of shame the morning after. I'm better than that. I don't do one-night stands or shallow flings. If and when I meet someone I intend it to have some meaning a bit deeper than a quick tumble in your bed.' She shrugged. 'Plus I'd like to be able to live in the same flat as you without things getting awkward. I'd like to have coffee with you or go running with you without any tension. I don't need any hassle in my life.'

Hassle? He stared after her as she headed for the bathroom.

'Where does that leave us, then?' he called, just before she shut the door on him.

'Exactly where it did before,' she called back. '*Flatmates*, Alex. I'm going to take a shower and get back to work.'

He hadn't expected a knockback. Mainly because they never happened.

From his room he could hear the shower running, his mind insisting on imagining her naked curves wet and covered in soap bubbles, and then various doors opening and closing as she returned to the boxroom, changed clothes and left the flat, presumably on her way to the shop. He lay on his bed with his hands clenched, his entire body a coiled spring of latent sexual tension. He could still feel the full softness of her top lip between his own, could imagine the creamy silk of her bare thighs beneath his hands. And kicking around the empty flat was making him feel worse by the second.

He left his room for the bathroom, showered, dressed and headed for the front door. What the hell? There were plenty of other single women out there who weren't workaholics.

CHAPTER FIVE

SO MUCH FOR fresh air and exercise aiding productivity. Lara had spent the past few hours shoving Alex Spencer and his delicious kiss firmly out of her mind only to find him right back there again five minutes later. Which only made her even more furious with herself when she eventually returned to the flat to discover the woody scent of his aftershave still lingering in the bathroom and no sign of him in the place. Based on what she knew of him, there was only one explanation: Her knockback a few hours earlier hadn't fazed him one tiny bit. He'd simply refocused his efforts in the usual direction. He'd clearly gone out on the pull.

Why did it bother her so much?

The churning deep in her stomach felt an awful lot like disappointment. Had she really been hoping that the interest he'd shown in her—moving fittings around for her in the shop, cajoling her into taking time out—might stem from genuine liking and concern? It was plain as day that what he really was hoping to gain from it was an easy lay. She should never have expected anything else and she didn't have time to spare to be sucked into this stupid debate with herself.

Poppy was making toast in the kitchen.

'No Alex?' she said, smiling as Lara walked in. 'You two seemed to be getting on like a house on fire.'

Lara shook her head and uttered a light laugh.

'No, he's just been giving me a hand shifting stock, that's all. I don't think he wants to get to know me beyond flatmate levels. Plus he seems to have a crazy social life and I'm up to my eyeballs in work.'

She could hear herself gabbling, protesting too much, and forced herself to stop before Poppy picked up on it. She had absolutely zero interest in how Alex Spencer was spending his evening. She crossed to the counter and concentrated on putting the kettle on.

Poppy sat down at the table.

'I'm not sure his social life is all it seems, to be honest,' she said, nodding her head as Lara held up a mug with a questioning expression. 'He's been through a lot these last few months.'

Lara busied herself, getting together instant coffee and milk from the fridge.

'You mean his injuries? He hasn't really mentioned them.'

Poppy shook her head.

'He wouldn't. He wouldn't let anyone fuss over him, even when he was in the hospital. He doesn't want sympathy, thinks that should all be directed at the soldier who lost his life. The lad was younger than Alex, such a waste.' She looked up at Lara. 'You have to understand his army mates were like family to him. I think that made it a lot harder. He feels responsible.'

Lara's mind reeled with the information. What exactly had Alex been through?

'It's not just the physical injuries. To him they're part of the job. He accepted that risk when he signed up. If anything, leaving the army seems to have been more of a wrench.'

Lara nodded.

'He did mention he was looking for a new direction. I tried to brainstorm a few work suggestions for him.'

Poppy stared at her in surprise.

'Did you? It's more than he's let any of us do.'

And what exactly did *that* mean? That he was interested in what she had to say? Her heart gave a tiny and poorly judged skip because it was a far more likely scenario that Lara was too pushy and hadn't let him get a word in.

'Just because we come from a big family doesn't necessarily mean there's a big support network going on there,' Poppy went on. 'And it's especially difficult for Alex when it comes to army stuff. My father's had an incredibly successful army career, really full-on stuff. He works for the United Nations as a military advisor and that's meant a lot of travel over the years, for him and for my mother. Alex and I had a nanny when we were very young, then boarding school when we were old enough. Alex went from school to university to Sandhurst then straight into the army. He had his whole life mapped out—right from the get-go he knew where he was heading and he seemed happy with that. He threw himself into army life, climbed the ranks at breakneck speed. It was like he was born to do it.' She gave Lara a rueful smile. 'In a way I suppose he was.'

Lara looked down at her coffee mug.

'He can be a bit gruff sometimes but don't be too hard on him. His whole life has changed, his whole future, and not through his choice. I'm not sure he's having an easy time coming to terms with that—that's partly why

I offered him the room here. The last thing he needs is my father harping on about military careers when Alex has had to give his up.'

Fresh air and exercise had also failed epically at living up to the promised restful sleep. One ear cocked for the expected arrival of Alex with unnamed conquest, furious with herself for actually being *interested*, Lara finally dropped off somewhere in the small hours. And now her alarm was going off, it was still dark and it occurred to her as she stared one-eyed at her own haggard reflection in the bathroom mirror while she brushed her teeth that she'd been so preoccupied with Alex's behaviour the previous day that she'd forgotten today's plans involved moving her stock from the flat to the shop.

Stock that was currently being stored in his bedroom. Where he was, presumably, holed up with whatever conquest he'd managed to pull the previous night. She might not have heard him make it home but that didn't make her any less certain he was in there. And since he had the most erratic sleep routine of anyone she'd ever met, he could sleep in for *hours* yet.

She didn't have hours. Time was, as usual, of the essence. She couldn't just tiptoe around him; she had work commitments. That the thought of seeing him in bed with another woman made her feel icky had absolutely no place in the debate, and she crushed the unhappy churn in her stomach as she walked down the darkened hallway.

She paused outside his bedroom door. Should she knock? On one hand it would be the polite thing to do, but then again it was only just coming up to six o' clock in the morning. October mornings included pretty full-on darkness at this time. Surely it would be far easier and much quicker to just tiptoe into the room and start by taking the stock nearest the door, mainly stuff that was boxed. She could leave the big clothing rails and the boxes near the window until later, when hopefully he would be up and his bedroom companion had been dispatched.

She held her breath and pressed the door handle down, eased the door open a crack and crept into the room.

As sleepless nights went, it made a change to be kept awake by something other than nightmares or sex.

Alex had undertaken his usual strategy the evening before, and he'd had no trouble finding company in the bar he went to. He never did. Unfortunately the rest of the evening hadn't panned out in the usual way. Engaging in conversation was even more wearing than usual and, worse, he seemed to have no real interest in where the evening was heading. He felt antsier than ever and the company just wasn't cutting it. At a little past midnight he'd made his excuses and returned to the flat. Alone. And sleep had eluded him ever since.

That Lara had knocked him back needled at his pride, yes, but it wasn't just about the snub. Nor was it the physical pull of her. She was very pretty, of course, and the girly, glamorous clothes she chose with her curvy figure and creamy skin really did it for him. It was both those things but more than that too. He *liked* her. More than he was used to liking someone. She had a zest for life that was intoxicating to him in this limbo state he felt so trapped in. She had her own goals, her own standards, without reference to anyone else's. And she made him feel as if he could have that too.

Somewhere before dawn, as he was finally drifting

towards dropping off through sheer exhaustion, he heard the bedroom door snick open.

The dim light from the hallway lit her up in silhouette and her light perfume drifted across the room, putting his senses right back on standby.

Lara was creeping into his room under cover of darkness and surely there could be only one explanation why she might do that. Perfectly understandably, she'd spent the rest of yesterday having second thoughts about knocking him back, probably followed by a sleepless night, and now she'd decided to take matters into her own hands.

He watched, his eyes completely accustomed to the darkness, since he'd been lying in it for the past five hours. She tiptoed to the side of the bed, and, really, was that her best attempt at stealth?

There was a clatter as she caught her foot on one of the wretched metal clothes rails and then a moment later a muffled yelp as she fell over a box. And then she picked herself up and paused, obviously gauging whether she'd woken him or not. He saw her head on one side in the semi darkness, as if she was listening closely.

In one swift movement, he leaned up from the bed, caught her around the waist and pulled her into his lap. Waited for her to melt into his arms as he groped for her mouth with his, his whole body firing up with hot anticipation.

Instead of the anticipated breathy sigh she let out an anguished squawk that wouldn't have gone amiss on a throttled parrot and karate-chopped him in the neck.

Thirty seconds later and Lara had disengaged herself from him, scrambled across to the light switch and snapped it on, all the while hideous thoughts tumbling through her mind of threesomes and goodness knew what else. She stared across the room at him as he blinked in the bright light, sheets pooled around his waist, super-toned naked torso, short hair lightly dishevelled. And she couldn't stop herself exclaiming in surprise.

'You're on your own!' she said.

Alex, sitting at the scrubbed kitchen table in a T-shirt and shorts, held up two fingers as she spooned instant coffee into a mug for each of them and she rolled her eyes as she added a second spoonful for him.

'No wonder you're perpetually awake,' she remarked.

'Yeah, well.' He looked at her over the rim of his coffee mug as she handed it to him. 'My sleep pattern may have become a bit…' he paused '…off balance since I got back. And don't change the subject. What the hell were you doing sneaking around my bedroom in the small hours if you weren't planning on jumping my bones?'

Was there no end to his arrogance when it came to women?

'I can't believe you'd just assume that,' she said.

He continued to look at her, eyebrows raised, and she took a big sip of her coffee.

'I was coming in to get my stock,' she said. 'I want to start taking it over to the shop today. There's still so much to do to get the shop ready before Thursday and I've still got to organise food for the launch evening to hand round with the pink champagne but I haven't even looked at it yet.' She sighed. 'I'm sorry I woke you. I was trying to be as quiet as I could.'

A herd of elephants might have a better line in stealth than she did, in his opinion.

'You didn't wake me,' he said shortly. 'I couldn't sleep.'

'Even without a...' she paused to pull a disapproving face '...*companion*, you're still awake half the night? Don't you *ever* sleep?'

He had absolutely no desire to discuss his sleep patterns with her or anyone else.

'And there was no need to sound so damn shocked,' he carried on, ignoring the question. 'I don't bring women back every night.'

She was watching him steadily, eyes narrowed.

'And even if I did, I don't see that there's anything wrong with that. We're all consenting adults.'

She shrugged, not meeting his eyes, but her body language screamed disapproval.

'Whatever floats your boat, I suppose.'

'What's that supposed to mean?'

She tipped the rest of her coffee down the sink and put the mug in the dishwasher. He could literally see her disengaging from the conversation.

'Nothing. Just that having disposable people in my life isn't really my bag. To me it just seems like a horrendous waste of time. Time I haven't got to spare.'

'That's because you obviously haven't had a *disposable person* in your life who's any good,' he countered, holding her gaze until he saw the blush climb up her cheekbones. Nothing was easy with her. He couldn't remember coming across someone who felt so damned challenging and it was clear that talking the talk wasn't going to cut any ice when it came to impressing her. He'd have to try a more practical approach.

He stood up and walked round the table towards her and rinsed his mug out at the sink. The heady floral scent of her French perfume made his senses reel.

'Come on, then,' he said, leading the way back to his room. 'If you need to get your damn stock.'

'Back to bed, is it, now?' she called after him.

'Well, I'm hardly going to get any sleep now with you clattering in and out, am I? Tell me what needs shifting and I'll give you a hand.'

His third navigation of the narrow stairwell and of all the bloody people to bump into when he was loaded down with boxes of knickers.

Isaac slung his duffel bag over his other shoulder and stared.

'You're back, then,' Alex said, stating the obvious.

'What the hell are those? And that?'

He pointed out the clear polythene clothes cover hanging over Alex's arm, through which peacock-blue satin and feathers were visible.

'It's a negligee,' Alex said. Since he'd moved in with a gang of women it felt as if a whole new world of vocabulary had opened up. 'And these are ladies' knickers.'

'Seriously?' Isaac pulled a shocked face. 'I leave the country for a couple of weeks and suddenly you're the authority on women's underwear. Is there something you're not telling me?'

For Pete's sake.

'I'm moving some stock for the girl who lives downstairs. *Lived* downstairs,' he corrected. 'She's taken Poppy's boxroom. Long story. She runs an underwear shop.'

Lara chose that moment to back out of the flat door behind him with an armful of lacy bras.

'Lara, this is Isaac.'

She nodded at him, squeezed past them on a cloud

of delicious perfume and disappeared down the stairs. Isaac watched her go.

'I take it all back,' he said, clapping Alex on the shoulder. 'Nice work.'

'It's not like that,' he said. He was beginning to wonder what the hell it *was* like.

CHAPTER SIX

LARA HAD DECIDED on a pale pink fitted dress that she'd designed herself, hoping it would hit the right note of old-school Hollywood glamour, and teamed it with heels that would kill her feet after a couple of hours but which gave the perfect impression. Drinks and nibbles were laid out on a temporary table in the middle of the shop, fairy lights were in place and switched on, lending a soft girly note to the shop floor. Every item of stock was lovingly hung or folded in exactly the right place. Fliers had been distributed everywhere she could think of. All that was left to do now was wait, and hope she would be buried in the rush of customers.

Her stomach was a knot of tension as she unlocked the shop door and positioned the stand-up sign on the pavement outside. The pink and black helium balloons fastened to it bobbed in the evening breeze.

She leaned back against the counter. Nothing yet. Worry began to gnaw at her insides that this had all been a crazy idea, that she'd sunk her entire savings into a venture that would never get off the ground, no matter how hard she worked. She struggled to crush it back down as she stared at her perfect but deserted shop floor and then Poppy and Alex were sweeping into the shop, followed by a couple of other fire-station residents. Two minutes later and a group of women dressed for the office crowded in, clearly on their way home from work. She noticed Alex pouring champagne into glasses and managed a smile at last. Worry was gone, the shop was buzzing and she was on her way.

Poppy, standing in the middle of the shop, leaned around Alex and pinched a breadstick, dunked it in one of the bowls of dip and ate it. Next thing he knew she was standing still and staring at the table, which was covered in bite-size nibbles.

'You helped Lara with the food?'

She stared at him with an incredulous expression and he ran a defensive hand through his hair. Somewhere along the line, helping Lara shift a few boxes of stock had graduated today into collecting a case of sale or return champagne and helping her organise the food. After all, what else did he have to be doing? Lying in bed staring at four walls? Walking or running aimlessly around Notting Hill?

'No, not really,' he evaded.

'Don't deny it! That's your signature dip. The one with the secret recipe that you always said you'd take to the grave.' As if to confirm it to herself she fumbled another breadstick from the pot and used it to lever an enormous scoop of dip into her mouth.

He shrugged and grabbed a cheese tartlet so he wouldn't have to look at her knowing grin.

'What's the big deal?'

'No big deal. Just that the last time I clocked your views on Lara's lingerie business you weren't quite so enthusiastic.' She took a sip of her pink champagne. '*Tart's boudoir*, wasn't it?' she said.

He looked at her in exasperation and saw the smile on her face, knew she was teasing. She touched his arm and leaned in.

'She's lovely, Alex. Makes a nice change.'

'Yeah, well, it would do. Except it's not like that. We're friends.'

She waved across the shop floor at Izzy, who'd just arrived.

'God knows what you've been doing traipsing round half the bars in Notting Hill as if your life depended on it,' she said with ill-hidden disapproval, putting her empty glass down. 'Friends is a bloody good start.'

Question was, would friends be enough?

He had to hand it to Lara: she was good at what she did.

He'd watched her for the last half hour, moving effortlessly from customer to customer, greeting people with a smile as they entered the softly lit shop from the cold darkness of the street outside. Nothing was too much trouble. Determination to make the venture a success was obvious in her every move.

'So you can offer tailored running classes?' the dark-haired woman at his elbow said. 'Would that be as part of a group or is it on a one-to-one basis?'

He tore his eyes away from Lara, who was holding up a raspberry lace vest and smiling on the other side of the shop.

'Either,' he said distractedly.

Whatever Lara had said at the playground, she'd obviously given him a great sales pitch. He'd been inundated with thirty-something women asking him about personal training, certainly enough inquiries to demonstrate that he could have a viable business here, if he chose to pursue it.

It felt vaguely against the natural order of things to be handing out his phone number to women when he had no intention of going to bed with them. Exhausted with their questions, he glanced around for an escape route and realised Tori had entered the shop while he was preoccupied. Just what he needed. She couldn't have timed it better if she'd tried. He immediately excused himself from the crowd of women, and headed straight over to her via the counter, where he took a couple of fresh glasses of pink champagne.

She looked up at him as she flipped randomly through the clothes rail near the door.

'You look tired,' he said, handing her one of the glasses.

Truth be told he was quite taken aback by the change in her demeanour since he'd last seen her at Izzy's house party. That had been over a month ago now and she'd been full of enthusiasm about her fabulous new boyfriend.

'Just for future reference,' she said, taking an enormous slug of champagne, 'when you say "you look tired" to a woman, what she actually hears is "you look like crap".'

He laughed.

'You don't look like crap. You never have.'

She raised her glass in acknowledgement. She was the life and soul of every party she ever went to and yet here she was looking through the rails by herself in the corner. Even the stripes in her hair seemed less vibrant than usual. He'd known her long enough to pick up immediately that something wasn't right. Maybe there was trouble in paradise.

'You've got it bad,' Tori commented.

He stood back a little.

'Got what bad?'

She gave him an exasperated look.

'Lara,' she said, making his stomach do a crazy back-flip. 'I've been watching you for the last five minutes. For Pete's sake, Alex, we've known each other since we were kids. I've got eyes. I can tell.'

'How can you tell?'

'You mean besides the fact you're actually *attending* a party in a ladies' knicker shop? Let me think…' She tapped one finger against her jaw in an exaggerated gesture of consideration. 'You can't take your eyes off her. And last time we met you tried to resurrect our friends-with-benefits agreement but you haven't so much as given me a second glance so far tonight. Don't suppose you want to revisit that conversation now?'

He had absolutely no inclination whatsoever to do that. And having it pointed out to him brought any delusions about how much he liked Lara crashing down around his ears. He had zero interest in pursuing Tori, or anyone else for that matter. Tori was waiting for an answer, an expectant look on her face. *Awkward.* He spread his hands apologetically.

'Tori, I'd love to but—'

She punched the air in a gesture of triumph.

'There you go. I rest my case.'

For all the jokey posturing he still thought for a moment that there was a hint of disappointment in her smile, but of course he had to be mistaken. She'd made herself quite clear at Izzy's party. Mark was, for her, the real deal. The *benefits* part of their friendship was, for her, well and truly over with.

'It's not like that,' he protested. 'She thinks I'm only after one thing and, to be perfectly honest, I'm not sure I'm up to offering more than that right now.'

He could see from Tori's smile that he wasn't fooling either of them. They'd always had an easy confidence like this; he knew he could trust her.

'I'm damaged goods, Tori,' he said at last. 'I don't want to put that on her.'

He watched over Tori's shoulder as Lara crossed the shop towards them, smiling and chatting to customers, working the room like an expert. Tori moved a pace sideways to block his view and grab his full attention.

'That's such crap, Alex,' she said. 'Damaged goods? For Pete's sake, everyone has a past. We've all got baggage, and you've decided that she'd make a judgement call about yours without even *asking* her opinion. That's really not fair, is it?' She turned away from him and began flipping through a rail of pastel silk dressing gowns. He watched as she rejected each one. 'Take your time, get to know her properly and show her there can be more between the two of you than just sex,' she said. 'You're here, aren't you? Offering support, helping her out. I'd say that's a step in the right direction.'

Lara finally reached them and Tori dropped her voice quickly and held up a short pink silk nightie.

'Have you got anything…*edgier*?' Tori asked her.

After a while smiling made your cheeks ache, and it really should come a lot more naturally based on the fact the launch was turning out to be a fantastic success. The turnout was brilliant, the buzz around her stock delighted her, and she'd already made lots of sales.

Lara caught herself looking over at Alex yet again and dragged her eyes back to the counter, forced herself to focus on processing the sale and talking to the customer. He'd made a real effort on her behalf this last couple of days, while taking great care to keep things on a friendly level between them. No more flirting or invading her personal space. She'd begun to wonder if he was trying to impress her, somehow show that she meant more to him than his usual conquests, maybe even prove that his interest in her went beyond disposable fling. Helping her shift her stock, for example, even pitching in with the catering. She hadn't expected that, hadn't expected him to *cook*, for Pete's sake!

Now it seemed that all he'd been doing was passing the time because, let's face it, he had nothing better to do.

He'd spent the early part of the evening surrounded by prospective fitness clients; she'd picked up snippets of the conversation herself every time she walked past him and she was secretly delighted at his new positivity. He'd also turned out to be a brilliant side attraction to her designs. Note to self: keep a hot guy on the shop floor at all times to maximise female footfall. And then somewhere in the last twenty minutes or so, Tori had arrived, and suddenly networking for a prospective fitness business seemed to have gone out of the window. She could see them in her peripheral vision, talking quietly, in each other's personal space. They obviously knew each other *extremely* well.

And that was when the unhappy churning in Lara's stomach had kicked off.

Now Tori stood at the counter paying for a beautiful

but undeniably racy basque and French knickers set in black silk, decorated with intricate lace and feathers, and some lace-topped silk stockings.

Poppy, looking on, sighed wistfully as Lara wrapped the delicate garments in pink tissue paper.

'It must be lovely to have someone in mind when you buy this kind of thing,' she said. 'They are *so* beautiful. Not that I need anything like that.' She nodded towards the nightwear rail on the other side of the shop. 'I'm going to buy a pair of those silk pyjamas.'

'They're so gorgeous, aren't they?' Tori said. 'Not that there's any point in me looking at them. Silk pyjamas would be a bit run of the mill for Mark's taste, no matter how lovely.' There was a resigned edge to her tone. 'In Mark's opinion, the saucier, the better.'

'All of this is for Mark's benefit, then?' Alex said, joining them.

Lara's stomach gave another twist at his obvious interest in Tori's relationship. First he'd spent ages talking quietly to her in the corner and now this. Try as she might to deny it, maybe dismiss it as first-night nerves, deep down she knew perfectly well what it was and she might as well face facts.

She was jealous.

'How are things with Mark?' Concern showed on Poppy's face. 'It feels like we've hardly seen you recently. Is everything OK?'

'Of course!'

Tori's smile was a little too broad, her tone a little too light-hearted to really sound genuine. Poppy was waiting for her to elaborate, as she always did. Instead she simply handed over her credit card to Lara. For the first time in history, it seemed, Tori was reluctant to talk about herself.

* * *

Lara's feet ached inside the skyscraper heels but she couldn't have cared less. Poppy had left a while ago with Izzy, each of them carrying a pink and black ribbon-tied carrier bag. Tori had disappeared back home to Mark. But even after all the potential fitness clients had gone, Alex had stayed. From beginning to end he'd been there for her shop launch, not giving it a miss or dropping in for a grudging half hour or so because she'd cajoled him into it. His support had gone above and beyond a favour. With the shop launch occupying every spare space in her mind, she hadn't allowed herself to consider what, if anything, *that* might mean. Maybe he was just being polite. Maybe he had nothing better to do.

It was full dark now outside and cold, a little past nine. She supposed he would go straight on to the pub now. Or the bar. Or wherever it was he disappeared to during his evenings out. The thought brought a twist of disappointment, which had no place amid her euphoria at the way the evening had gone.

She focused her mind on her work. All that was left to do now was tidy the shop and cash up. Alex carried the pavement sign in from the darkness of the street.

'Thanks for all your help today,' she said, crossing to the counter breezily to avoid looking at him. 'It's been a fantastic success. You can get off now. I'll just cash up and tidy round a bit.'

The shop floor seemed suddenly still and quiet after the buzz of the evening. His voice came from behind her.

'I'll stay while you lock up and then I'll walk you back.'

So she'd been wrong about him finishing the evening with his usual routine. Her stomach gave a slow and deliberate flip at that throwaway comment and what it might mean if she let it.

'There's no need.'

She heard his exasperated intake of breath.

'It's pitch dark out there and I assume you'll be carrying your takings? Don't argue.'

She moved around the shop, tidying up. Just turning the sign on the door around to read 'Closed' gave her a spark of happiness. This was *her* business, *her* shop. She'd worked so hard for this evening and it had gone well. She was acutely aware of him beside her as she cashed up and put the takings in her bag. He made her feel protected, cared about, and that touched her on a level she rarely allowed anyone to reach. She'd allowed that to happen, of course, accepting his help when she took help from no one. There was danger inherent in that, but she'd believed herself immune to it because she wasn't interested in the quick shallow flings he favoured. Now he'd moved the goalposts, his usual routine and line-up of conquests interrupted, and as a result her opinion of him was no longer such a great defence. Watching him with Tori had shown her she liked him a lot more than she admitted, to him and to herself.

Now that some of the stress of the project had been alleviated her consciousness of him seemed to have increased a hundredfold.

'It's been a huge success,' Lara said. Her eyes sparkled and she looked absolutely radiant in the soft pink lighting of the shop. Alex's heart turned over softly. He waited while she flicked the shop lights off and locked up and then she was next to him, walking the icy pavement in the clear night air.

'You seem to get on well with Tori,' she said after a moment.

His interest sharpened instantly that she'd even noticed.

'I've known her a long time,' he said. 'She used to come and stay with us in the school holidays when Poppy and I were kids.' He paused. 'We've dated on and off over the years. Actually, not even dated really, more ended up together when both of us happened to be free. Nothing heavy.'

She uttered a little laugh.

'Nothing ever *is* heavy with you, is it?'

He considered that for a moment, dug his hands deep in his pockets as they walked.

'You have to understand what my life was like, in the army. I was away so much, and I put so much of myself into it that there wasn't much left for anything or anyone else. And it's a very regimented way of living. For as long as I can remember I've had someone else to answer to—be it a housemaster at school or a senior officer. Suddenly having all this freedom was weird. I could do whatever I wanted, whenever I wanted. I'd had years of heavy. I decided to make up for lost time.'

Silence for a moment.

'So is that what you were doing? Tonight with Tori. Making up for lost time?'

His heart was picking up the pace tentatively.

'No, we were just catching up. That side of things was never such a big deal and it's in the past now. We're friends, nothing more.'

'Because she's with Mark?'

'Not just that, no. What's with all the questions?' He

threw caution aside with a throwaway comment that he could pass off as a joke if he needed to. 'Jealous?'

'No!'

Her immediate sharp denial told him all he needed to know and tendrils of hope began to climb through him.

A pause.

'Just interested,' she qualified.

'It might have escaped your notice but I haven't been out with anyone recently, Tori included. It's kind of lost its charm.'

'Why's that?'

'Isn't it obvious?' he said, exasperated at last by the interrogation. 'Do you think I make a habit of hanging around ladies' clothes shops? Don't you think I'd rather be out at the pub right now, keeping it simple? I've spent my whole life answering to other people, living by the rules, and these last few weeks have been the first time in my life I've been free to live it up without regard for anyone else. And now I find I don't bloody *want* to. I'd rather be chatting to a gang of women and drinking pink champagne if it means being with you.' He stared up at the sky. 'What have you done to me?'

For a moment there was silence and he chanced a glance sideways. She wasn't looking troubled or as if she was gearing up to give another rendition of her rejection speech. She was smiling up at him and that was all the encouragement he needed. He stopped walking, tugged her into his arms and kissed her.

His room back at the flat was channelling its usual sparse military as Alex crossed the room to close the curtains. The soft glow from the bedside light highlighted the ordered shelves and perfectly made bed.

'This room is in dire need of soft furnishings...' Lara began as he moved back towards her, and then he stopped her mouth with a kiss and all thoughts of décor disappeared from her mind like smoke. He cradled her face in both hands, his thumbs stroking her jaw softly as he caught the curve of her lips in his, easing them apart and caressing her with his tongue. Sparks of heat spread slowly through her body to melt in her stomach and tingle between her legs. His shoulders were huge and broad, tightly muscled. She let her hands slide up his chest and around his neck, let her fingertips slip through his hair as he curled huge arms around her. Reservations about disposable relationships melted from her consciousness; they required presence of mind, and the all-encompassing force of her physical response to him had swept that away. Her past relationships had never stifled her ability to keep her head, not like this. What was it about him that made her rational mind switch off?

Her perfume filled his senses.

It was like unwrapping the most decadent of luxury gifts. Layer by gorgeous layer, velvet, lace, silk, crystals. He found the zip at the nape of her neck and slid it smoothly down to the base of her spine. The silk dress slipped easily from her shoulders and fell into a soft gleaming pool at her feet. Beneath it he found a slip so thin it was almost translucent. The soft glow of the lamp on his bedside table gave her skin a creamy sheen against its peach silk and he caught his breath. He was used to living in the roughest of conditions and everything about her exuded luxury, the decadent scent of her skin, the soft slinky fabrics unfamiliar beneath his fingers. There was a femininity about her that was so intoxicating it made his senses reel.

He slipped the thin straps of her slip off her shoulders, and followed his progress with soft kisses, tracing her collarbone, moving lower. Her skin was as smooth and flawless as the silk clothes she wore. Beneath the slip there was a delicate lace bra, and he moved his lips across its roughness to suck her nipples gently through the gossamer-thin fabric. She moaned softly and arched her back, and desire surged through his body at her reaction. He slipped the straps of her bra off her shoulders as her fingertips found the buttons of his shirt and pushed it from his shoulders, then she slid her hands lower to tug the button of his jeans, remove them and free his erection. Her fingertips played lightly over his length, making nerves flutter softly in his groin, and he caught her hand before he could lose control. Curling an arm around her waist, he lowered her to the bed, and there she lay before him in the soft lamplight, the beautifully cut bra and knickers highlighting her curves perfectly. Her underwear was made to be seen, and he found her self-confidence in her body intoxicating.

He let his hands play over her body, exploring, revelling in the hitch of her breath as his fingertips found the silky skin of her inner thighs, in the tensing of her body as he teased his fingers beneath the soft lace of her panties, stroking her apart and then sliding two fingers inside her. She gasped against his neck as he found the sensitive nub at the very core of her and circled it lightly with his thumb as his fingers picked up a deliberately slow rhythm. With his free hand he cupped her breast, pinching the hard point of a nipple lightly between his fingers, pushing her slowly higher until she tensed against him as she found her climax.

A moment passed as she lay curled against him, and

then she tipped her head back and found his mouth with hers, her tongue slipping softly against his, firing him up even further. Then she leaned upwards, moving above him, her blonde hair silky against his cheek as her lips moved to his neck. Then lower still. He failed to stop himself tensing as her kisses strayed towards the ruined skin on the left-hand side of his chest, his fists clenching tightly at his sides. He hadn't given it a thought before, hadn't cared what any of his partners since the accident might think about him.

She mattered.

She was so beautiful, so perfect, and the thought that she might find him repellent filled him with sudden dread.

Her progress didn't falter. The line of kisses continued softly over his chest as if the twisted and puckered skin weren't even there. Relief washed over him, and with it desire for her that swept away all restraint. In one swift movement he turned her gently on her back, then leaned away briefly to find a condom in the drawer to one side of the bed.

Lara's heart thundered so fast and hard that she fancied he might hear it. As he slowly circled her slick entrance with his rigid erection she wanted him so much that she raised her hips from the bed, trying to take control and push him forward, yet he made her wait, teasing her until she thought she might cry out before he finally thrust forward, taking her in one deep fluid movement. His hands found hers on either side of her head, twining her fingers in his own as he found his rhythm, thrusting forward smoothly again and again, all the while holding her gaze with his own until she could hold back no longer and she cried her pleasure against his neck as he took her over that delicious edge. A moment later and his body tensed against her own as he followed her.

As her breathing evened she curled her body against him, tugging the blanket free of its perfect hospital corners and snuggling into him deliciously, already her thoughts breaking up into sleep.

Faint notes of her perfume still clung to her hair and Alex closed his eyes and breathed them in. Her fingers entwined in his, and he felt a sense of peace that had eluded him since he'd arrived home.

For the first time in weeks he didn't fight sleep when it came.

Big mistake.

CHAPTER SEVEN

IT STARTED WITH a couple of shivers as he lay next to her. Not enough to drag her fully back to consciousness from the delicious deep, sated sleep, but just enough for awareness of his presence to seep in, for the deliciousness of the previous evening to surface in her mind and make her stomach flutter before she sank back down into slumber.

And then there it was again. Soft muttering. This time she opened her eyes and frowned in the dim light of the very early morning. She was curled snugly against Alex, his arm curled protectively around her, her head nestled comfortably in the hollow beneath his jaw. She inhaled the warm, musky scent of his body. The feeling of warmth and safety warmed her to her toes.

She moved up onto one elbow and screwed her eyes up, looking down at his face in the semi-darkness with its strong bone structure. No longer pinned down by her, he suddenly flailed his arms and shouted aloud, making her jump, and she scrambled into a sitting position. Her mind backtracked madly to the day they met—had it really only been a week or so ago? He'd fallen asleep in her flat while she worked. His sleep had been disturbed then too.

She leaned across and clicked on the lamp on the bed-

side table. Deep in sleep, he didn't wake. And little wonder—he was clearly so sleep-deprived that once sleep had
him in its grasp it wouldn't let go easily. Worry twisted
in her chest as she watched a frown cross his face. Beads
of perspiration shone on his brow. Muttering kicked back
in, louder this time. Vague, garbled words, none of it in-
telligible.

Unable to bear the anguished twisting of his body
a moment longer, she reached a hand out to shake his
shoulder, and when that didn't work she began patting
his cheek lightly.

'Alex?' she ventured.

His arms flew back against the headboard and a strangled shout that was leaning towards a scream left his lips.
In a panic, Lara did the only thing she could think of.

The dream had Alex right in its dark grasp, fear and despair pelting through his veins as he staggered through
the smoke, tasting its acrid bite at the back of his throat
as he tried to call out for Sam, desperately searching for
him and for their driver.

And then a sudden flood of icy coldness dashed full-
force into his face and he was scrambling to sit up, dis-
orientated, water dripping from his face onto the sheets.
He screwed his eyes up and tried to focus in the unexpected bright light.

'What the hell…?' he spluttered. The fragments of the
dream were still whirling in his mind, his heart pound-
ing thickly in his chest.

His eyes slowly began to adjust. Poppy's flat. His bedroom. Present day. Lara was sitting a few feet away from
him on the bed, the sheet clutched against her chest, the
empty glass from his bedside table in her hand and an

apologetic look on her face that did nothing to mask the underlying fright.

'I tried shaking you,' she said apologetically. 'You were muttering in your sleep and thrashing about. Nothing worked. And then you really shouted and I kind of acted on reflex.'

Her voice trailed away. Her hair lay in loose waves over her bare shoulders and her china-blue eyes were wide with worry. She looked utterly beautiful and hideous shame boiled through his veins as he comprehended what had happened. Making love to her had lulled him into such a state of euphoric hope that he'd stupidly thought he might have beaten off some demons. What a fool he was for thinking he might have turned a corner with his nightmares just because Lara was in his bed. What the hell must she think of him, crying out in his sleep like a baby?

His flailing mind chose that moment to treat him to a hideous memory of his father, one of thousands of similar memories, berating him as a seven-year-old for crying as he was decamped back to school yet again. His face burned in spite of the cold water that still clung to his cheeks. Emotional displays were shameful, something to be avoided at all costs, and avoiding them had become second nature. When he was awake. Apparently his unconscious self still needed a few lessons in self-control.

He attempted to joke his way out of it.

'Your reflex reaction is a bit sledgehammer-to-crack-a-nut, isn't it? Remind me not to get on the wrong side of you.' His hair was damply sweaty as he ran a hand through it.

She didn't smile. Her pretty face was full of sympathy,

fuelling the humiliation all the more. He couldn't bear to have her pity him.

'What's going on with you, Alex? Is this to do with your injuries? The roadside bomb? Poppy mentioned how difficult it's been.' She put her hand on his arm gently. 'You can talk to me, you know.'

'You've been discussing me with Poppy on the quiet?' Mortification kicked up another notch.

'Not in a negative way,' she said. 'She was concerned about you, that's all. She could see we were becoming friends.'

'It's nothing to do with Poppy or anyone else,' he snapped. 'There's nothing to talk about.' It came out more strongly than he'd meant it and he caught the tiny recoil on her face. She took her hand away and cut her eyes away from his. He forced his voice into a light tone. 'So I had a bit of a disturbed night—I probably drank too much at the launch. No big deal.'

He avoided her eyes, instead swinging his legs off the bed and putting on shorts. The silence in the room was heavy with tension. He needed to get out of here for a few minutes, calm down. Then when he came back the moment would be over with.

'I'll be right back,' he mumbled, heading out to the bathroom.

Lara watched the door close behind him and gritted her teeth against the wave of miserable disappointment churning in her stomach. Two words: *Unrealistic expectations*. Had she really thought that after his romantic declaration of feelings for her, followed by the most unbelievable stomach-melting night, things might actually be rainbows and butterflies from now on?

No. But it might have been nice if they could get past the morning after before her hopes were dashed. She of all people should know better than to expect more. This was *her* life after all. Rainbows and butterflies had never featured before—why the hell should they be putting in an appearance now?

Her mind was working overtime. There was more to this than a one-off or a glass too many of pink champagne. From what she'd seen and heard of him last night he certainly hadn't drunk that much. Her thoughts kept going back to the unsettled sleep he'd had back on the sofa in her flat. And now something else clicked into place in her mind. His major overuse of caffeine. The odd hours he kept—sleeping in the daytime, up and about half the night. Try to palm this off as a one-off or a phase, he might, but she knew better.

Whatever this was, he apparently didn't have enough regard for her to be straight with her about it. And really—was that such a big ask? She pushed her fingers back into her hair, trying to think clearly. The way he'd helped her with the launch, their growing friendship, the way he'd been with her last night. Had all that just been a stepping stone to bed after all? Had he just upped the ante after she'd knocked him back after their run, playing the game, pretending he wanted to get to know her until he got what he wanted? Anything deeper than that was apparently not on the agenda.

Self-preservation kicked sharply in and she threw the covers back from the bed. She padded quietly around the room, picking up her clothes, finding her shoes, all the while squashing the feeling of hurt stupidity for thinking there might be more to this than just sex.

* * *

In the bathroom Alex filled his palms with cold water and held them against his face, wondering how the hell to play this now. He could kick himself for falling asleep. So wrapped up in the deliciousness of having Lara cuddled up to him, he'd relaxed for once, not even sparing a thought for his nightmares. He was filled with hot shame at what he might have done or said in his sleep; it had certainly disturbed her enough that she'd lobbed water over him. In any other situation it might have been funny.

His immediate reaction was to back off. At speed. He'd intended to have fun for a while, not to get in so deep with a girl that he actually cared what they thought of him. In getting to know Lara he'd somehow lost sight of that objective. The sensible thing now would be to draw a line under the whole thing. Go back to being nothing more than neighbours who made small talk. Yet the thought of not seeing her again except in passing, of just being acquaintances, made his stomach lurch with disappointment.

He gripped the edges of the sink and looked down at his hands. He would have to find another way to deal with this instead of ending it. He just needed to put in a bit of distance. His best option was surely to fob her off, dismiss the nightmare as one of those things, and then find a way to make sure it didn't happen again.

He took a deep breath as he walked back down the hall and pushed open the bedroom door.

She was dressed. Or at least dressed enough to indicate the night was well and truly over. She wore her pink frock from the launch party and the beautiful undergarments hung over one arm. Her shoes were in her other hand. Worse, her face was full of disappointment. Clearly in him. And who could blame her? Had he really assumed she would still be interested in him after this? Naturally being woken up to his girly screaming had put her off.

'You're leaving,' he said, stating the obvious. His stomach churned with despair at the realisation that he'd blown this.

'I should never have stayed,' she said. 'Last night was a mistake.'

'There's no need for you to go,' he said quickly. 'I'm sorry if I overreacted or scared you. It was just a dream, just one of those things. This doesn't normally happen.' OK, so that was stretching the truth more than a little but he'd worry about that later; if he had to stay awake twenty-four-seven from now on to hide his weakness from her then he would manage it somehow. He held a hand out to her. 'Come back to bed.'

She rolled her eyes at the ceiling.

'So you want to dumb down this whole thing between us until all it's about is sex,' she said. 'I don't know why I'm even *surprised*.' She took a step nearer the door, then turned back and flung a hand up in a gesture of exasperation. 'It's not the bloody *dream* that's the problem. It's your reaction. It's the way you've just fobbed me off and then suggested bed as if sex might just divert me from getting to know you on any deeper level than that. *A bit of a disturbed night?* It was way more than that. And you can try and pass it off as a blip or a one-off if you want, but I'm not an idiot. This isn't the first time it's happened, is it? What about when you fell asleep back in my flat—you had a nightmare then too, didn't you? And that's why you're always trying to stay awake. Why didn't you just say you're having trouble sleeping? Don't you think I *care* about that?'

He groped for an answer that wouldn't make him look a total arse. He'd thought he'd got away with the sleep disturbance in the flat that day. She'd never mentioned it since. It felt suddenly as if he were under the spotlight and defensiveness kicked in.

'What is this—twenty questions?'

Disappointment filled the blue eyes at his curt tone.

'No, this is me wondering why you're not being straight with me and realising I already know the answer. You said it yourself the other day. You've never been with a disposable person who's any good. That's how you see yourself, how you see this, isn't it? A quick fling. OK, you might have had to jump through a few extra hoops this time to get your way, but you got there in the end, didn't you? Like an idiot I thought there might be more to us than that.'

She headed for the door while he stared after her in horror, seeing how the conclusion she'd reached must look so obvious to her in the light of his previous behaviour, his string of one-night-only girlfriends.

'There *is* more to us than that,' he called after her.

She paused. Turned to look back at him from the open doorway.

'OK, then, prove it,' she said. 'Sit down with me now and be straight with me about what just happened.'

He stared at her, groping for something to say that would turn the situation around and failing. Because he knew exactly what she'd think of him if he sat down opposite her and told her all about his night terrors. About the bomb blast and his broken promise to look out for a nervous soldier who looked up to him. About his failure to be of any use whatsoever to those whose safety was ultimately his responsibility. The silence yawned between them until she shook her head.

'I've got work to do,' she snapped.

The door clicked shut behind her.

It didn't have the best flouncing-out value when you were only going feet away down the hall but she'd given it her all anyway, cutting her eyes sharply away from him and slamming the door behind her. At least the walk of shame was only a few paces. Bloody Alex. She should be euphoric after yesterday's success but instead she was filled with stomach-wrenching disappointment.

Back in the boxroom she sank onto the narrow bed and rubbed her scratchy eyes with her fingers. The clock on the dresser told her it was a little before six. Five minutes later and she was heading into the shower, mind forcibly refocused back where it should have been all along. Her work.

Coffee in Ignite accompanied by an enormous *pain au chocolat* that would undoubtedly go straight to her hips, then she would head in to open the shop. She ate it anyway, because the size of her hips was irrelevant now that she wasn't intending to get naked with a man again any time soon. Had to go and sleep with him, didn't she? She should have known better. She stared at her laptop screen and focused hard on updating her blog with photos from the launch. Anything to crush the feeling of stupidity, and the underlying prickle of concern for him that he really didn't deserve, because however hard he might try to brush it off those nightmares were no picnic.

Somehow the concern was worst of all because it told her she actually *cared* about him.

Try as she might to concentrate on writing a blog post, her eyes kept wandering to the door. Which of course was insane because he hadn't exactly beaten the box-room door down upstairs to try and talk to her. She'd heard nothing from him from the moment she slammed his bedroom door. And why would she? It all fitted. He'd got what he wanted—why would he want anything more to do with her? The only difference between her and all his other walk-of-shame girls was that she'd slammed the door on the way out instead of kissing him goodbye.

As she polished off the last of the pastry, not really wanting it but grimly eating it out of principle, the door of the café opened and her stomach gave a disorienting flip. She bit her lip hard enough to hurt because her eyes might have been glued to the door but she hadn't for one moment thought he actually might walk through it. He crossed the room towards her via the counter, where she heard him put in his usual order of coffee strong enough to strip wallpaper. And then he came to a standstill next to her table, by which time her heart was thundering so loudly in her ears that it was a wonder she could hear him when he spoke.

'I'm sorry,' Alex said.

Her hair was loosely tied at one side, curling over her shoulder, and the porcelain cheekbones were without their usual touch of colour. She looked tired and frag-ile. *His fault.* A prickle of guilt spiked inside him and he wondered briefly if it would be better to just leave her be instead of subjecting her to his attempts to move on with his life. Then Tori's words from the previous evening flit-ted through his head. *We've all got baggage, and you've decided that she'd make a judgement call about yours without even asking her opinion. That's really not fair...*

Lara looked up at him, pen clenched in one hand, face carefully neutral. Her posture was stiff and guarded, giving nothing away.

'For what?'

'For everything. Can I sit down?'

A pause. And then she nodded at the opposite chair. He pulled it out and sat opposite her, looked down at the table for a moment, gathering his thoughts, then looked up and into her cautious blue gaze.

'I know how it looks, but you're wrong,' he said. 'This is not just about a one-night stand or a quick fling for me. I told you that last night and I meant it.'

She held his gaze levelly, giving nothing away.

'But that didn't make it any easier for me to tell you about my nightmares. What the hell would you have thought if I'd dropped in a quick warning before we went to sleep? If I'd told you that I might freak out somewhere in the small hours? You'd think I was a complete nutter.'

He looked back down at the table.

'Truth is, I'd had such a great time last night that for once I didn't stress about going to sleep. I didn't think I could have a nightmare when I was feeling so…well, so relaxed.'

He glanced up to see her expression soften a little. He tried hard not to see it as a sympathy look. If he did that, he might not be able to continue.

'I haven't told anyone about the dreams. Not even Poppy. I didn't want to worry her. It's my problem, no one else's and I'm dealing with it in my own way,' he said.

The counter girl chose that moment to walk past and place a supersized mug of black coffee in front of him. He nodded his thanks as he took a huge slug of it, relishing its strong bitter taste and waiting for the buzz to kick in and sharpen his senses.

She nodded at the mug, a cynical expression on her face.

'That's you dealing with it your own way, is it? Over-dosing on caffeine and avoiding sleep.'

'Short-term management,' he said. 'In actual fact things have improved. Already the dreams are getting less frequent, I just need to give it more time.'

Not strictly true. They were less frequent because he *slept* less frequently. But he had no wish to undermine the improvement by analysing it too deeply. He was convinced he just needed to give it time. Surely the longer he spent out of the army, the less he would dwell on it, right?

'What are they like? The dreams?' she ventured. Her voice was tentative, as if she was worried he might snap at her.

His stomach churned a little at the question. Verbal-ising what happened hadn't really been on his agenda when he'd come to find her; he'd simply hoped to apol-ogise and talk her round. But here it was, his chance to prove he was totally on top of this. Totally in control. He gripped the mug of coffee hard in one hand and curled the other into a fist, forced what he hoped was an I'm-in-total-control-of-this neutral expression onto his face.

'They're always the same,' he began, keeping it short. Keeping it *vague*. That was best. 'The explosion, the heat and the smoke. And then this awful sense of disorienta-tion.' He dug his fingernails into his palm and glanced around the café. Chatting customers, background music, *reality*. 'And then I wake up.' He forced a grin. 'Or in this instance, I *get* woken up by being dunked in cold water.'

She smiled back, but the smile was a size too small.

'You scared me half to death,' she said.

'I'm sorry.'

She shook her head slowly.

'It must have been an awful time for you. I can't possibly imagine what it must be like to have that in your head. Have you had any counselling? Don't they offer that kind of thing?'

'I'm not some basket case,' he said defensively.

She rolled her eyes.

'I'm not suggesting you are. I want to help, that's all. I want to understand. I'm not passing judgement.'

He wasn't about to confide in her beyond the most basic level. Better by far to keep things simple between them, to keep it fun. For neither of them to get too attached. Wasn't her independence part of what was so attractive about her? She had her own life, her own agenda that had absolutely nothing to do with him. She was far too preoccupied with her own goals to really *need* him and he found that so appealing about her, that she demanded sole responsibility for her own life.

'I thought you of all people would understand that this is something I want to handle myself,' he said.

An indignant frown touched her eyebrows.

'What's that supposed to mean?'

'Miss I'll Shift My Own Furniture,' he said. 'Didn't you tell me you hated relying on anyone else's help?'

A grin twitched at the corner of her mouth and his spirits lifted. He pressed on.

'Is it so wrong to try and get through it myself first before I drag anyone else into it? It wasn't a personal judgement about you—I haven't told *anyone*.'

'No, it's not so wrong.'

He covered her hand with his, noticing she didn't pull her fingers away.

'Does that mean I'm forgiven?' he said.

She looked up at him through narrowed eyes.

'Depends.'

'On what?'

'That you don't try and hide it from me. Or anything else, for that matter. I need you to be straight with me. And you stop trying to stay awake twenty-four-seven.'

'Anything else?'

'You buy me another pastry.'

'Done.'

CHAPTER EIGHT

NORMAL COUPLE. HE COULD do that. In those early days when he'd left the army, keeping it casual had been the automatic choice. Freedom to go where he chose, when he chose, with whomever he chose had held a novelty value that was intoxicating after the years of rigid structure in his life. Yet throughout that time of shallow one-night stands and partying, he'd found no real sense of satisfaction. There had still been that uncomfortable sensation of being rootless, of having no direction.

Now he understood why. When it came down to it, he had missed it. The sense of *belonging* that school and the army had provided. He only truly realised that now he was beginning to regain it. He revelled in the sense of direction that the new business gave him, in the steadiness that living with Poppy offered, and now in the happiness that being with Lara brought. Casual really wasn't him. He had a sense of moving forward now instead of living a disposable, inconsequential, limbo life, and he wanted that feeling to stay. Letting his relationship with Lara become steadier was the inevitable next step.

Now that things were sorted between the two of them he felt more certain of that than ever, confident that he'd taken another step towards building a normal life outside the regimens of the army, putting the past further behind him. He'd been frank with Lara, right? Just a couple of nightmares and he was handling them himself, no biggie. Surely it was only a matter of time now before they disappeared completely.

Girlfriend—*check*. New and promising fitness business—*check*. Place to live that had no bearing on his past—*check*.

A group of people were just drifting into Ignite for wine and tapas as Alex passed them and climbed the stairs to the flat. He'd just finished his very first personal training session—up until now it had all been about assessing fitness levels and planning exercise schedules and diets. Now he'd actually embarked on proper fitness sessions with a couple of clients. Things were moving forward. With every step he insisted to himself that life was back on the right track.

The laughter and chat could be heard as soon as he walked through the door and he followed it to the kitchen. Isaac was sitting at the table, leaning back in his chair with a grin on his face, Poppy was busy at the stove, whirling a huge wok around, and Lara was at the counter opening a bottle of wine.

'You're back again, then, mate,' he said to Isaac, crossing the kitchen and sweeping Lara's blond hair to one side so he could kiss her cheek.

Poppy made retching sounds from the other side of the kitchen.

'What are you, twelve?' he asked her. 'Just because you're perpetually single.'

She shot him a look and turned back to the stove. Lara held up a wine glass and raised her eyebrows but he shook his head and crossed to the fridge instead for an energy drink. Wine was not a good option if you wanted to disprove all suspicion of sleep deprivation. He'd end up falling asleep at the kitchen table.

'How did it go, then?' Lara said. 'Your first full-on personal training session.'

In his experience commanding soldiers was infinitely easier. For a start they didn't question his authority or answer back. Or stop to reapply lipstick. Yet at the same time he couldn't deny it was nice to actually have a sense of worth and purpose again. OK, so it might only be short term, he hadn't absolutely decided where he might go with it yet, but at least he was earning now. At least he could feel he was moving forward. And the more he thought about it, the idea of running some kind of boot-camp-style class was really appealing, dealing with groups of people at a time. Maybe he could try it out on adults first and if that worked think about pitching the idea to schools.

'Challenging,' he said. 'Having my orders questioned at every turn is a new and interesting experience, but yeah.' He shrugged. 'On the whole it went well.'

'I thought I'd cook,' Poppy said. 'Since you've got your first session to celebrate. And Isaac's back, of course,' she added as an afterthought, glancing at him. 'We haven't had a group meal since Izzy left. I'm doing Thai green curry, fragrant rice and a slaw. Lara's bought cakes from the café and Isaac…'

'I've got the drink angle covered,' Isaac said easily. 'Pull up a chair.'

Poppy dished the curry up into huge bowls and joined them around the table.

'How long you staying this time?' Alex asked Isaac, forking up some rice.

Lara noticed Poppy glance up sharply at him from her

plate. She could see how it might be annoying that Isaac essentially treated Poppy's flat like a hotel. Things had changed quite a bit now from when Lara had first moved into her studio flat downstairs. Izzy had still been living with Poppy; Tori had been forever dropping in; there were constant parties and girly chats.

Isaac shrugged.

'Couple of days. Depends what comes up.' He winked at Lara. 'No two days are ever the same. I'm heading to Blue later. You should all come along.'

'Blue?' Lara said. What the hell was that?

'Isaac's bars have a colour theme,' Poppy supplied. 'Blue is in Islington.'

'How long have you all known each other?' Lara said. Isaac only seemed to stay over the odd night, despite the fact he was obviously stumping up for the rent. How lovely it must be not to have to think where every penny was coming from. It was clear he and Alex got on like a house on fire. Although, glancing at her, she didn't think Poppy looked quite as comfortable.

Isaac leaned back in his chair, swirling white wine around his glass.

'I've known Alex and Poppy for years,' he said. 'Alex and I were at school together. I used to crash at their place every school holidays. You've no idea the dirt I could dish on the pair of them.'

Out of the corner of her eye, she saw Poppy visibly tense at that comment. Next thing she was on her feet, heading to the fridge with her back to them. She returned to the table with a bottle of water.

'Dirt?' Lara said.

Isaac shrugged easily.

'Nights out, holidays, that kind of thing. Trip of a life-time to Las Vegas.'

'Hah, you're so funny,' Alex said with tones of deep-est sarcasm. She threw him a questioning look and he flung up a hand. 'I blew half my inheritance on an ill-judged week away with him and the guys. Let's just say Lady Luck wasn't in my corner in the casinos.' His tone was throwaway.

He might as well be speaking in some kind of for-eign language. Lara had zero comprehension of a world where there was such a thing as an inheritance, let alone a swanky holiday to blow it on.

Isaac topped up their drinks, hovering the neck of the wine bottle briefly over Poppy's glass as she put her hand over it. The camaraderie between him and Alex meant the kitchen was full of laughter as they reminisced. By the time the meal was finished Lara had built up a pic-ture in her mind of a rich childhood and adolescence, of an enormous country pile in the Cotswolds, of posh holidays and a friendship group, all of whom were too cool for school. With every anecdote she felt more and more like a fish out of water. At last Poppy stood up and began clearing plates from the table.

'Want some help?' Isaac offered.

'That's OK, I've got it,' Lara said quickly, getting up. Relief surged through her that the meal was over, closely followed by irritation at herself for being so bothered. This wasn't school. She wasn't the perpetual new girl anymore. Why should she even care whether she fitted in here or not? Living in Notting Hill was a strategic career move, not a popularity test. She opened the dishwasher and started stacking crockery.

'In that case—' Isaac looked at his watch '—I'm heading into the city. The night is young and all that. Anyone want to come along?'

Poppy shook her head immediately.

'I'm on duty in an hour,' she said. 'Night shift. I need to get moving.'

'You go,' Lara said. 'I'll finish clearing up.'

'Laters, then,' Isaac said, holding a hand up and heading out of the door. Moments later the front door of the flat slammed behind him. Poppy headed to her room to get ready to leave for work.

Alex cleared the glasses from the table as Lara wiped the surfaces.

'You were quiet,' he said.

'Was I?' She kept her back to him as she stood at the counter. Her life was a whole different ballgame from his. Apart from the fact they happened to have ended up in the same flat, they had absolutely nothing in common. Their lives were literally miles apart. How could she possibly expect to fit into his world once the first flush of novelty wore off? An unhappy prickle of doubt climbed her spine. How long could a relationship survive before those kinds of fundamental differences started to cause cracks?

'Yes, you were.' He moved across to her at the counter, and tugged her by the hand to sit down next to him. She could see the concerned expression on his face. 'What's up?'

She pitched her tone of voice at light, hoping to make it look as if it really weren't such a big deal. *That's it, Lara. Shrug it off.*

'Your upbringing was just so different from mine,' she said simply. 'Yours and Poppy's. Big family, loads of relatives, friends down for the holidays.' She paused. 'It was just interesting, listening to you all talking about it, reminiscing. I couldn't really relate to any of it.'

He shrugged.

'Yeah, well. It had its downside too,' he said shortly. 'What about you, then? You haven't told me much about your background. Except that your mother taught you how to sew, didn't she?'

'Not my mum. Not exactly,' she said.

She smiled cautiously back at him and took a sip of her wine.

'Foster mum,' she corrected.

'You were fostered?'

He sat up straight; she'd spiked his interest now. Her background had had the ability to do that when she was a kid too. In many a school playground she'd been a new and interesting life form. New starts were hard.

'My mum was very young when she had me.' She watched for his reaction. 'She was only fifteen, just a kid.'

To his credit he didn't flinch, so she carried on.

'She tried her best but she just couldn't look after me properly. It wasn't that she didn't want to, she just didn't have any support. Her own parents weren't much help.' She shrugged. 'Long story short, I ended up being taken into care.'

His face was full of concern and her stomach lurched a little despairingly. So far he'd only seen strong Lara, independent, driven Lara who made things happen for herself. She didn't want to be seen as weak or in need of sympathy.

'And then you were fostered?'

'I was.'

'What about your father?'

She shook her head. *Who?*

'I never knew him. I'm still in touch with my mother, we see each other now and then, but we're not close. We never really had a chance to be. I don't blame her. She had everything working against her and she wasn't much more than a child herself. I didn't have any brothers or sisters, like you have Poppy. It's always been just me.'

'What was your foster mother like?'

Which one? For Lara, there had only been one who mattered. The others didn't deserve a mention; they barely even registered for a thought.

When she thought of that time, the time when she'd at last felt settled, the smile came more easily. 'Her name is Bridget. I went to live with her and her husband and they were lovely. Warm and friendly. Bridget was the one who taught me how to sew—she'd worked for years as a seamstress and she was brilliant at it. She made all her own clothes, toys, soft furnishings, you name it. Up until then I'd drifted through life with no real direction and then suddenly I found something I was good at and someone who was actually interested in me.'

She thought back to the hours she'd spent learning how to shape seams, put in darts, sew button holes. Bridget's endless patience with her stream of questions. The enthusiasm for her new skill that almost bordered on greed in her eagerness to learn more, practise more. 'My whole business has stemmed from there. I did a costume design course at college, got some work experience, then started making my own stuff.'

'Are you still in touch? She must be really proud of you.'

She nodded.

'I see them when I can. Talk on the phone, and visit,

that kind of thing. When I hit sixteen and went to college I moved out of their house and found a room to rent. I started building up my own life, looking out for myself, and I've been doing that ever since.'

Alex watched her as she swirled the wine slowly around her glass. Had he ever come across someone so independent, so determinedly self-reliant? It gave a very attractive sense of security to what was happening between them—he was comfortable in the knowledge there was no way her happiness and well-being could ever be totally dependent on *him*. No need for him to worry about things stepping up a notch between them because he knew she could manage perfectly well—and perfectly happily—without him.

'So you can see it was a bit like an alien world to me, listening to you and Poppy and Isaac chat through your childhood,' she said. 'I didn't really know how to engage with that. We're really very different, you and me.'

He could tell by the tone of her voice that she didn't consider that to be a good thing.

'Your childhood sounds idyllic,' she carried on. 'You were so lucky growing up, having this massive family, financial security, a big country home.'

He couldn't hold back a cynical laugh.

'Yeah, well, it might look Pollyanna from the outside, but it's really not.' He lobbed aside his reservations about alcohol and sleep and poured a splash of wine into an empty glass for himself. 'I don't think security and happiness is about having blood relations, not really. Poppy and I are up to our ears in relatives but scraping the bottom of the barrel when it comes to support and family love.' He smiled at her frown. 'Money helps, of course, but up until now I've never been brilliant with that. I got my inheritance at the same time as Poppy but it's mostly gone now. She was the sensible one, investing it in bricks and mortar. I never really thought ahead that far—my whole life revolved around the army. I never thought for a second I might need the money for a back-up plan. Instead I frittered it away on holidays with the lads, lost a whole load of it back there in Las Vegas—Isaac wasn't joking about that. All in the name of fun.'

He looked at her small, indignant face. She'd been up against so much as a kid and she'd triumphed in the face of it. He couldn't help but be impressed by that kind of tenacity. He'd had all the financial trappings and foot-in-the-door family reputation that anyone could want to get him ahead in life. Just look how far she'd got without any of that.

He reached out across the table top and took her hand in his.

'You've pushed yourself to get where you are and that's something to be proud of—you didn't get there on the strength of your family name or your father's reputation. When you look at your business and your shop, at everything you've achieved, you know that you've done all of that on your own. The credit's yours.' He paused. 'I wish I could say that.'

'You can. You were a captain in the army. They don't just hand things like that out on a plate.'

He shrugged cynically.

'I come from an old military family—we go way back. My father has contacts at the highest level. I'd be a fool to think my family's reputation hadn't helped me get where I am.' He paused and swallowed. 'Where I *was*. Unfortunately it doesn't count for much anymore. And since I left the army any interest I did have from my family has melted away. Do you know that since I left hospital my parents haven't visited even once?'

Was it worse, Lara wondered, having all that prospective love and support just sitting there but having it withheld? How was that better than not having it at all? At least she knew where she stood. There was no disappointment because she had no one to be disappointed *in*.

'I guess what I'm saying is that you and I are not so different,' he said. 'It might seem like that on the surface. I've got relatives coming out of my ears and you've got none to speak of, but mine are completely useless. They have nothing to do with my life, no interest in me. We might come at it from different directions, but basically both of us are on our own.'

He downed the glass of wine in one and stood up from the table, his face set. Saying it out loud dragged it out from the recesses of his mind and the familiar taste of bitter disappointment rose in his mouth. For the longest time he'd had institutions in his life to replace what his family lacked. First school, then university, then the army. A circle of long-term friends to give that feeling of belonging. The floundering feeling he'd experienced in those first weeks after discharge from the army, the rootless feeling that he was going it alone, made an unwanted comeback. He'd made inroads since then, settling into Notting Hill with Poppy, finding Lara, finding a new direction in his business plans. The last thing he needed was to revisit that pointlessness.

She looked up at him with a questioning expression and he leaned over to smooth her hair back from her forehead and kiss the creamy softness of her brow.

'I'm going to take a shower,' he said.

Lara's rose-tinted view of his perfect upper-class

childhood felt suddenly skewed and her heart twisted a little for him as he left the room. She could tell he was unsettled. All those people in his life to support and love him were really people to live up to or to disappoint. She felt a new and unexpected affinity with Alex, a closeness that she hadn't realised was there. Maybe they weren't so far removed from each other after all. The thought of that brought a surge of heated desire for him deep inside her at a level beyond that provoked by his gorgeous face and his muscular body.

Without thinking what she was doing, she put the dish cloth down on the counter and left the kitchen to walk slowly down the hallway towards the bathroom. The strength of her need for him somehow transcended her usual presence of mind, breaking down her self-control. When had she ever let her guard down like this with a man, revelled in the physical deliciousness of being with someone unfettered by the endless thoughts of self-preservation by which she lived her life?

The thundering sound of water from the shower was audible from outside the door. She tried the door before knocking and it opened smoothly. With Isaac gone and Poppy at work until the morning, he clearly wasn't bothered about privacy. She was. The last thing she wanted was Isaac dropping back and bursting in unexpectedly. She closed the door behind her and twisted the spring lock.

The room was warm and the air heavy and damp with scented steam from the shower. It smelled fresh and spicy and made her heart skip into double time. The undeniably male shower gel, which he used as an antidote, he said, to all the pink and pretty girly toiletries that cluttered every surface in here.

Behind the steamed glass of the shower cubicle she could see the shadow of his huge shoulders tapering down to the tightly muscled torso. Heat began to course through her and pooled tinglingly between her legs. Slowly she stepped out of her clothes and padded barefoot across the cold tile of the floor to slide open the glass door.

She stepped into the shower unit beside Alex as if it were the most natural thing in the world and his initial surprise was quickly followed by a surge of arousal at her smooth nakedness. As the shower spray soaked her blond hair, darkening it, he slid his hands across her wet skin, circling her waist and pulling her tightly against him. He groped for her mouth with his, found it and crushed his lips against hers, hot need for her crashing through him. She knew exactly what she wanted from the moment and she took it on her terms. He found that completely mesmerising about her.

The masculine scent of his shower gel hung on the steamy air, citrus and bergamot filling her senses as she slid her hands over his soapy skin, feeling the rock-hard muscle beneath. He pushed her gently back against the wall, the smooth stone tile pressing cold against her shoulders and butt. His hands were everywhere now, exploring her, moving to cup her breasts, to hold them close together while he gently sucked their hard tips, sending dizzying sparks right through her to burn hotly between her legs.

Warm water sluiced over them as he moved slowly lower, taking his time, trailing a line of kisses softly down the hollow between her breasts, over her flat stomach and lower still. Kneeling before her now in the shower stall, he ran his hand down the length of her legs, and lifted one of her heels until her knee lay supported over his shoulder. Her legs were held firmly apart now, the better to expose her fully to his attention.

Lara leaned her head against the hard tile of the wall, the shower spray missing her face now, instead sluicing in a torrent down her body and over his. Nerve endings jumped and sparked between her legs as he kissed his way up her inner thighs, taking his time, making her wait. Then with one delicate stroke of his tongue he parted her swollen core and she heard her own sharp intake of breath as her head rolled deliciously back and her eyes fluttered shut. He found the sensitive nub and began to circle it softly with his tongue, one hand holding her against his mouth, the other first teasing lower and then sliding two fingers deep inside her in one smooth movement. He seemed attuned to her every response, moving his fingers in a slow and delicious rhythm, caressing her with his tongue until she felt herself climb towards that elusive height of sensation. Losing control, she curled her fingers into his dripping-wet hair and in response he increased his smooth pace until she cried her pleasure at the ceiling.

Before she could fold on her jellified knees into the bottom of the shower stall, waves of deliciousness still coursing through her, he'd slid the glass door of the stall open and grabbed a condom from the cupboard beside the sink. As the water thundered on in the empty stall behind them, he lifted her gently from the shower. Water splashed and pooled across the bathroom floor as he turned her to face the bathroom wall, clasping a firm hand around her waist, the other at her inner thigh. She felt the press of his rigid erection against her slick core and then he was inside her, filling her completely, taking her in long, slow strokes, his muscular torso firm against her back as he swept her wet hair aside and kissed the nape of her neck. The cold, smooth tile of the wall pressed against her hard nipples, her fingers traced marks in the condensation on either side of her face as she began to climb again. With him this time, feeling his breath quicken with every stroke he took. And as he finally tipped her back over that dizzying height of pleasure she felt him cry out his own ecstasy against her bare shoulder.

CHAPTER NINE

SHE LAY CURLED now into the crook of Alex's arm, in the soft pool of light from his beside lamp. His fingers entwined in hers, deliciously warm, sated and comfortable. Her things were starting to trickle into his room. Not much yet, just her robe and a few items of clothing. Funny how it felt like no big deal. Sleeping with Alex every night was spared full-on scary seriousness because she had her own room just down the hall and a separate shelf in the fridge. Not to mention a flat just downstairs that should be ready to move back into in a day or two. Outside the door the flat was quiet; there was no sign of Isaac returning. Then again, by the sound of it, when Isaac partied he didn't do it in small measures.

She frowned a little as she thought of Isaac, recalling Poppy's behaviour at dinner.

'Poppy seems a bit tense around Isaac,' she commented. 'Is there something going on between them?'

She felt him shake his head.

'She seemed OK to me,' he said. 'Fab scoff, as per. She's always been a great cook.'

'Typical brother, you are,' she said, exasperated. 'Completely oblivious. You could have put the atmosphere in that kitchen through a mincer. And Poppy couldn't get out of there fast enough. Honestly, men are so insensitive sometimes.'

He laughed softly into her hair.

'I can be sensitive when I want to be,' he said. She looked up into his grey eyes as he shifted in the bed, turning her gently and leaning up on one elbow to place an arm either side of her head. He tangled his fingers in her hair and kissed her so tenderly she thought her stomach might melt. She wrapped her limbs around his body, loving the fact that he was so tall and broad-shouldered, so heavily roped with muscle. She felt protected. Warm and safe. It wasn't just in the way he was with her in bed, it was in the little things he did, in not allowing her to walk a couple of streets home in the dark, in stepping in to move furniture around for her.

It was a sensation she wasn't used to experiencing, had in fact *avoided* feeling, instead substituting the need for it with her own drive and ambition. Letting herself relax into feeling safe had been something she'd learned to avoid growing up because it usually preceded the figurative rug being jerked out from underneath her. The feeling of contentment, of trusting someone else with her feelings, was something she'd learned to be wary of. She was older now, though, and wiser. She had her own life well and truly under control, providing for herself without the need for anyone else. She told herself this thing with Alex, whatever it was, didn't need to have any detrimental effect on that.

As sleep began to break her thoughts up she cuddled into him and let her guard slip a little. She could afford it.

Alex lay against her, breathing in the sweet scent of her hair in the darkness as she nestled her head beneath his chin, and stared at the ceiling. Through sheer will he held his eyes open, grimly refusing to let the comfort and warmth of his bed, of Lara curled against him, drag him into sleep. He wouldn't be making that mistake again. He listened as her breathing evened and gradually let the stroke of his fingers against the silky skin of her bare shoulder slow until it stilled. She didn't flinch. The room was silent.

Then he added on another twenty minutes just to be sure.

When he was certain she was fully asleep he shifted her gently from his chest and waited quietly while she snuggled into the pillows, then he moved across to the edge of the bed. Smooth, slow movements so as not to disturb her. There was no tripping over random items on the floor or bumping into furniture. When it came to moving in the darkness with stealth, Lara could learn a thing or two from him. He closed the bedroom door quietly behind him and headed to the kitchen, his laptop and a large mug of strong black coffee.

There was a surprising amount of admin and red tape associated with starting up a small business, even a fledgling one like his. At first the personal training thing really hadn't been much more than a way of buying some time, perhaps earning a bit of money while he decided on a proper new direction. Not to mention a way of keeping Lara and Poppy off his back with their seemingly endless career advice and suggestions of how he should be spending his time. Yet this last week, having taken his first couple of one-to-one clients out, talking through their hopes for weight loss and improved fitness and formulating a tailored fitness plan for each of them, he'd been surprised at how enthusiastic he was about the whole

venture. Already he was planning to trial group running classes, and after that possibly week-long intensive
boot-camp-style courses. The possibilities were endless.

Unfortunately there was more to it than spending all
his time outdoors handling the practical one-to-one fitness stuff. There was advertising to think of, public li-
ability insurance to consider; he needed to record his
income and expenses. The list went on and on, and Lara
had been impressed at his organisational skills, not knowing of course that he'd had hours to spare for designing a
website, setting up accounting software, scouting around
online for the best insurance deals.

When you slept less than four out of every twenty-
four hours it was amazing how much you could get done.

Lara was so tired from her in-your-face working day
that once asleep there was no waking her until her alarm
went off at some godforsaken dark hour of the morning, and at which point she would leap out of bed and
the whole damn work routine would start all over again.
The last few nights he'd been able to slip back into bed
shortly before her alarm, simply getting back up again for
an early run as soon as she was up and about. He sched-
uled his fitness clients in the morning, usually after nine
when the school run was out of the way, and before lunch.
Then he would grab a few hours' sleep in the afternoon
while Lara was occupied at the lingerie shop. By the time
she was finished he was up and about and she was none
the wiser. And that way, he could limit any sleep disturbance to when she wasn't there.

Lara would be able to move back into her own flat in
days, now that the plumbing was fixed and the replas-
tering of the water-damaged wall was under way. That
would take the pressure off even further. After over a

week of sharing each other's living space, that would be a step back. Staying together all night every night would likely become less of an automatic choice. Just a few more days of managing his routine and it would be easier.

In the meantime this was turning out to be the perfect solution to his nightmares. Squeeze them out. If he gave them as little opportunity as possible it stood to reason that they would happen less, that they would relinquish their grip on him. There had been no sleep disturbance at all for the last two days. And so the strategy, complicated though it was, appeared to be working. Until he could be sure he was rid of the nightmares, he intended to rigidly control his sleep pattern. Whatever it took to achieve surface normality, he was prepared to do it. Hope began to grow at last in his heart that the whole hellish experience might finally be behind him.

Isaac expertly popped the cork from the bottle of Perrier-Jouet to the background sound of cheers and claps filling the sitting room. Lara had never met anyone before so adept at producing like magic the perfect bottle to suit any occasion. She wondered if he kept a stack of bottles hidden away in his room, ready to whip out with a flourish when required. Relaxed shared flatmates' dinner? Chilled bottle of Pinot Grigio. Announcement of former flatmate's whirlwind engagement? Top-notch champagne, nothing but the best would do.

He filled flutes one by one as Poppy held them out to him.

'I bloody well told you so!' Poppy said triumphantly, passing a flute first to Alex, then to Lara. 'Didn't I say that ring on Izzy's right hand was fooling nobody? Finally she puts me out of my misery and moves it to the correct finger.'

Lara could see excitement on Poppy's face mingling with a measure of relief that things had obviously worked out so wonderfully for Izzy. She looked blissfully happy with Harry's hand resting around her waist. Lara offered her own congratulations as she examined the swirl of silver on Izzy's left hand.

'It's beautiful, Izzy,' she said. 'Just so elegant.'

A pang of unexpected wistfulness surged through her stomach as she examined the ring, silver with a couple of diamonds, gorgeous in its simplicity. Not wistfulness for the ring, gorgeous though it was, but for how lovely it must be to have someone make that commitment to you, to be able to look forward to a shared future instead of a solitary one.

'Izzy and Harry,' Isaac said, raising his glass. They all followed suit.

'How's your father doing, Harry?' Alex asked.

Harry smile tightened almost imperceptibly.

'On the mend, thanks,' he said. 'Touch and go for a while back there but he's over the worst now. I guess we'll see when we go back in a few weeks for the wedding.'

There was an immediate shocked gasp from Poppy.

'*For the wedding?* You mean you're getting hitched in Australia, not here? You can't!'

'We're doing both,' Izzy said, smiling.

'Both? How's that going to work?'

'We're getting married in London first,' Harry said. 'Something more intimate, so Izzy can have all her friends and family there, and then we'll decamp to Australia afterwards for the full-on "official" take on it.'

'So chill out,' Izzy said, 'no one's going to miss out,

you'll all be there. And actually, Lara, can I have a quick word?'

Izzy drew Lara quietly to one side as Isaac refilled glasses.

'I was wondering if you'd consider making my wedding dress?' she ventured.

A flush of genuine pleasure warmed Lara's cheeks. She was thrilled to be asked, to be trusted with such an important part of their day.

'Seriously?'

'Absolutely. Your lingerie is just gorgeous. And you do other clothes too, right, not just underwear? I'm right, aren't I? That dress you wore at the shop launch?'

Lara nodded.

'I make some of my own clothes, yes.' She clasped her hands together to contain her excitement. 'I'd *love* to do your wedding dress. It would be an absolute dream. What kind of thing did you have in mind?'

Lara sat down on the sofa and Izzy perched next to her, opening her tote bag and spreading a pile of wedding magazines out in front of her. As Izzy flipped through some cuttings Lara grabbed a pen and notepad and made notes furiously.

'I was hoping we could come up with a design that could double up for both weddings,' Izzy said. 'Nothing fussy, just simple lines.' She pointed to a magazine clipping of a full-length, elegant sheath dress, stunning in its simplicity. 'Kind of like this, but maybe with more of a drapey neckline.'

'Like this?' In a few strokes Lara sketched a draping column of a dress with a cowl neckline.

'Yes, exactly like that.' She clapped her hands together excitedly. 'I'm going to have an angora sweater for the service here—it'll be a very fine knit that I can wear over my dress. Hand-made. I've outsourced it to my mother!'

Lara smiled.

'And then the second wedding in Australia is going to be hot so I can just wear the dress without the sweater.'

'I'll put together some proper drawings for you and then we can fine-tune the design from there,' Lara said. 'I'll need to take full measurements from you. I'll need to know what shoes you're wearing, work out what lingerie will be best, that kind of thing. And we'll do fittings as we go along so we can make sure it's exactly what you want.'

'Perfect!'

Izzy's enthusiasm and excitement filled the room and another stab of envy poked Lara sharply behind the ribs. Izzy and Harry had been together for, what—a couple of months? And yet they were so utterly sure of each other that they were storming forward with wedding plans.

'It must be lovely to be so certain of something,' she said, before she could stop herself. 'Of *someone.*'

Izzy glanced up from the sketches and smiled.

'You're loved-up with Alex, aren't you?' she said.

'Of course.' Lara shrugged. 'But I haven't a clue really where we're headed. I've got so much on at the moment and the business always comes first. I don't have time to think about the future of any relationship. Not right now.'

Saying it out loud felt vaguely reassuring. There was a niggling sense of unease at her current situation that she'd tried hard to ignore. She hadn't counted on how happy it would make her feel, how secure, being with Alex. She looked across the sitting room to where he was joking around with Isaac, and her feelings for him bowled her over with their strong, confident depth. For the first time since her childhood she let her dogged tunnel vision slip and allowed herself to wonder if a solitary future really *was* the only option for her. There was no harm in dreaming, right? Maybe even in playing out the dream a little—why rule anything out? Surely Lara, with every aspect of her life under full control, could be open to seeing where this thing with Alex led without committing herself fully? In fact it would be odd if hopes and dreams *didn't* enter her mind right now—they were exactly what weddings were all about after all.

Mutual support. There was something deliciously couple-ish about it. Something that made Lara feel warm and happy deep inside, the unfamiliar sensation of being part of a team. Alex had been there for her at the shop launch, and now it was her turn to step up to the plate and return the favour.

Shame really that, in her case, mutual support had to include gruelling exercise. How much more palatable it would be if, for example, Alex ran a wine bar, like Isaac. She could quite happily envisage herself socialising, dressed in something sophisticated with a cocktail in her hand. She would be perfect for the role. Instead, here she was again, dressed in her mishmash of borrowed sportswear and bringing up the rear of a group of eight thirty-something women, all of whom looked a billion times more attractive than she did. Honestly, wasn't the whole *point* of needing to go to boot camp that you *didn't* already look your best?

This was Alex's attempt to diversify his test market from one-to-one personal training into fitness classes, leading a sample group of women on a cross-country run through the woodland of Holland Park. It had undoubtedly been preceded by one of his customary sessions of gruelling warm-up exercises and, possibly, instructions on how to keep up without turning into a sweating mess. Unfortunately she'd missed all that so she'd just have to wing it. She'd lost track of the time, sorting out loose ends at the shop instead of rushing here straight after closing. Alex had timed the half-hour run carefully to make the most of the last hour or so of daylight.

The woman directly in front of her had chestnut-brown hair caught up in a perfect high ponytail and co-ordinating pink and black designer sportswear. As Alex led them uphill Lara was treated to an unwelcome view of her perfect pert bottom emphasised by skintight leggings. Insecurity stabbed her sharply in the stomach and she grimly did her best to ignore it and plod on through the mud and leaves. Since the night of the launch, nearly a week ago now, Alex had been there for her on every level. He'd given her no reason to think he'd be interested in anyone else, no matter how good they might look in Lycra.

She made a special effort to pull her posture together, hold her head high and present a bouncy jogging motion instead of her body's default attitude of staggering along. Unfortunately holding her head high meant she didn't spot a sudden hollow in the squelchy ground preceded by a protruding tree root. Didn't spot it, that was, until her foot had caught in it and she'd performed a dying-swan sort of movement that ended in a muddy splat as she fell flat on her face. Mercifully, being at the back of the group meant no one realised she was floundering on the ground behind them.

The running group jogged on ahead of her in perfect unison, manoeuvring through the trees with Alex's voice counting out the pace in loud shouts from the front. Lara scrambled back to her feet as quickly as she could, only to fold immediately back onto her knees the moment she attempted to put weight on her left ankle. The pain was horrible, making her head spin and sending stars across her field of vision. She watched the group putting more and more distance between them.

The main path was only a few hundred metres away, the end of the run a short distance along it. The choice was perfectly simple. Either she could draw attention to herself as the weakest link in the team, distract Alex from his very first test class, which up until now had clearly gone perfectly to plan, or she could do her best to limp to the end of the course.

No contest.

In her mind there wasn't even a decision to be made. She attempted gingerly to test her foot again and bit her lip. Painful, but manageable as long as she didn't keep her weight on it for too long. She pulled herself grimly into what could only be described as a limping jog, concentrating hard on not falling too far behind the group, and forced herself over the final leg of the run. By the time Alex brought the group to a standstill at the finishing point, she was reduced to lurching along like a total moron. Fortunately he was so engrossed in leading the cool-down exercises that he didn't notice her limping appearance at the back.

She leaned against a tree a short distance away and closed her eyes briefly. The cool-down exercises could go to hell. With no weight on it her ankle didn't feel too bad. Perhaps she just needed to give it a minute or two to recover. She waved at him from the sidelines as he caught her eye, and watched him talk to his adoring class. She could hear him bandying motivational phrases around. And then as the class finally dispersed he made his way over to her, an exhilarated grin lighting up his handsome face.

'You made it,' he said. 'I thought you'd got held up at the shop.' Then, eyes narrowing, 'Just how late were you? Did you do the warm up?'

'Just about caught it,' she lied, taking the bottle of water he offered and sipping it gratefully. 'I thought the class went brilliantly, didn't you? Just wait until the word gets around at the school gates—you'll be inundated.' She pasted on a beaming smile.

He turned back towards the path, zipping up his hoodie, ready to get back to the flat. Dusk was beginning to fall now and the street lamps were kicking in. Lara tried her weight on her ankle carefully and pressed her lips together. The pain was monstrous. She gritted her teeth and limped along anyway a foot or so behind him, which was fine for a few seconds until he turned back and put an arm around her shoulders. Oh, the bliss of having something to lean on. She shoved her arm around his waist and used him as a crutch. And just a couple of paces was enough.

'What the bloody hell is going on with your foot?' he said, stopping immediately. She could hear exasperation fighting with concern in his tone of voice.

She drew herself up to her full height. Not easy when only one of your ankles could bear your weight. She pasted a breezy smile on her face.

'I slipped a bit on the way round. It's nothing.'

Totally ignoring her, he was already on his knees in the mud, loosening the laces of her trainer. She couldn't stop a yelp as he eased it off.

'Lara, it's swollen. When did you fall?'

'Near the end,' she said. 'Just when we turned back onto the main path.'

'That was way back,' he said. 'Why the hell did you keep going? Why didn't you stop the class?'

And make a total fool of herself in front of Notting Hill's yummy-mummy set? Did he know *nothing* at all about female pride?

'There was no need,' she said. 'I wasn't about to make a fuss and put a stop to the class, not when it was going so well.'

He slid an arm gently around her waist and took her other arm over his shoulder.

'Let's get back to the flat. With any luck Poppy will be there and we can get her to look at it.'

'I don't need Poppy to look at it, I'm perfectly all right. Don't fuss.'

He stopped then and looked her in the eye. She saw with some surprise that he was fighting to control his temper. Just what the hell was the big deal?

'Don't fuss?' he snapped. 'You were part of my class and that makes you *my* responsibility.'

'And how exactly are *you* meant to be responsible when I didn't tell you what I'd done?' she said. 'Nothing would have made me pipe up in front of that gang of middle-class mums in their DKNY sportswear that I'd just slipped in the mud in my too big cast-off trainers. I'm over eighteen, Alex, I'm not made of *glass*, and I don't need Poppy looking at my foot.'

'However you try and dress it up, I'm accountable for this,' he said, as if he hadn't heard a word. 'For you *and* your foot. So for once in your damned independent life, accept some help. This isn't a laughing matter. If I'm going to be running these classes professionally then health and safety has to be paramount.' He shook his head and frowned. 'Maybe I should have done another risk assessment.'

Oh, for Pete's sake.

'Can you just stop with the health and safety?' she said, holding up a hand. 'A thank-you might have been nice instead of a dressing down. Perhaps you'd like me to get down in the mud and give you fifty press-ups? Do you really think I *wanted* to turn out in the freezing cold and schlep round Holland Park? I came because I wanted to give you some moral support.'

He stared at her.

'I appreciate that, but I can't have *my* responsibility compromised because *your* mind isn't on the class,' he said. 'If you've just come along for a jolly and you're not going to take it seriously then it's probably best you don't come at all.'

A *jolly*?

Despite the rapidly cooling air, a rush of boiling heat suffused her from the neck up.

She disentangled herself from his arm, elbowed him aside and limped ahead at speed. The pain in her foot was awful but the way she felt right now she'd rather walk fifty miles on it than spend one more minute leaning on him.

'Lara, stop,' he said, jogging alongside to keep up with her. 'Let me help you.'

She stopped next to him.

'There was nothing *jolly* about hauling myself around Holland Park in the freezing cold,' she said through gritted teeth. She shook him off as he tried to take her arm. 'I wanted to be there for you, the same way you were there for me when I was biting my nails to the quick over my shop launch. But now I know you don't want me to bother unless I've got some kind of *fitness* objective, I'll stay out of the way in future. Risk assess *that*!'

She stormed off again and this time he didn't follow her.

CHAPTER TEN

ALEX LET HIMSELF into the flat and found Lara in the kitchen with her foot up on one of the chairs and Poppy strapping the ankle up with elasticated bandage. Lara's arms were folded and she had a mulish expression on her face.

'What happened to not needing Poppy to look at it?' he said, exasperated. 'You were having none of it back at the park.'

'Oh, she tried her best to limp past me,' Poppy said, glancing up. 'Lucky for you it isn't broken,' she told Lara. 'Just a strain. Take it easy for a day or two and it will be fine.'

He knew just by the expression on Lara's face that hell would be freezing over before she took it easy. Poppy covered the whole thing with a tube bandage and stood up to pack away her first-aid kit.

He could feel the indignant vibes radiating from Lara. The instant Poppy left the room she put her foot on the floor.

Alex had begun the solo walk back to the fire station fired up with exasperation at Lara for not taking better care of herself and, worse, with fury at himself for not being in better control of the class. How the hell had he not noticed whether she was at the warm up or not? Irritation gave way to thinking through the situation. This had been a test class after all, a chance for him to fine-tune the running of things. Maybe Lara had done him a favour. Better that he picked up on any loopholes like this now, before a paying client had some kind of accident on his watch. He resolved to tighten up his protocol before going any further with the boot-camp model. But then calm thought returned, and with it came a stab of guilt at the way he'd gone off at her. Lara Connor with her single-minded attitude, determined to run her life on her own without letting anyone in, had turned out to support him in his new business venture, a business venture that by the way she'd been instrumental in setting up. When did Lara ever make time for anything except her own business plans? Yet she'd made time to come and support him.

'How is it?' he asked.

'It's perfectly fine,' she said in tones of pure frost.

He pulled out the chair opposite and sat down.

'I'm sorry,' he said. 'I didn't mean it to sound like I'm ungrateful for your support—'

'But you'd just rather take the *personal* out of personal training,' she cut in. She held her hands up. 'It's fine. I'm *more* than happy not to come to any more of your classes.'

'It wasn't about not wanting you at the class.'

She simply stared at him with a sceptical expression on her face. *Yeah, right,* it said. He ran a hand uncomfortably through his hair.

'It wasn't actually about *you* at all,' he said. 'It's about accountability. You have to understand I've spent years taking decisions that affect other people. The army was all about that for me—having people rely on me, following my orders without question or thought for the consequences. It was all about not letting people down, because when you stuff up with that kind of thing in an army situation people get hurt.'

He knew that better than anyone. His mind sideslipped madly back to that final tour before he could stop it. Private Sam Walker looking at him with that half grin on his face. *'I know you've got my back, sir. And I've got yours.'* He blinked hard and forced himself to refocus on the present, on Lara. Her expression softened a little, the cynical slant melting away.

'You're not in the forces anymore, Alex,' she said patiently. 'Lives aren't at stake. You don't have control of what other people do or say. You can do all you can to make sure things are safe, and you're doing that. You've covered the insurance angle, you're up together on warm-up exercises and risk assessments. But you can't control the fact that I turned up late and bent the rules, or that my heart wasn't in the run. You can't take the blame because I screwed up. You're not responsible for the rest of the world.'

'You're more than just the rest of the world,' he said. 'I care what happens to you.'

A warm and fuzzy stomach flip kicked right in and Lara pressed her hands over her tummy hard. He *cared*. She was used to taking care of herself on every level, taking responsibility for every aspect of her life herself; his downright refusal to let her go her own way without voicing his concern was completely new to her. The sensation of being looked after, of being *cared about*, was one that she'd denied herself for so long that she'd forgotten just how lovely it was.

Or how dangerous.

What exactly was she doing here, letting herself get so close to someone that being *cared about* came into the equation? It was the living-in thing, of course. That was why it had slipped past her guard. Circumstance and not conscious choice had meant they'd ended up sharing a flat. And maybe it was the Izzy-and-Harry thing a bit too. Being part of the whirlwind excitement of their fairy-tale happiness made anything seem possible. The warm and happy feeling was intoxicating. Would it really be so dangerous to just run with this and see where it led?

When he reached across the table and covered her hand with his, she didn't take it away.

Two hours later and if she had to put up with one more minute of sitting still in the flat with a constantly re-filled cup of tea and a magazine, Lara thought she might scream. Not that she'd had any big plans for this evening except possibly to sort through some stock and then cook a meal, but now she was unable to do either of those things she felt hemmed in.

Still, when he appeared in the sitting room showered and changed she smiled at him through gritted, *bored* teeth because, actually, his concern was something she was liking very much. If only he could exhibit it in an-other way than ensuring her bladder stayed above the pint level with his endless cups of tea.

He smiled back, crossed the room towards her, and before she could make any comment he leaned down and picked her up from the sofa as if she weighed abso-lutely nothing. She was treated to a delicious wave of his aftershave, something woody and fresh, and she curled her arms around his neck immediately, her stomach beginning to fill with heat. Now *this* beat reading women's magazines.

'Where are you taking me?' she said in surprise as he failed to take the expected route to his bedroom. He kicked open the door of the flat and proceeded to carry her down the stairs.

'Ignite,' he said. 'I could see you were climbing the walls in there.'

'Could you?' she said, interested that he could be that perceptive.

'Yep. It was that tight voice you used when you thanked me for the tea.'

'I'm sorry,' she said, feeling guilty. 'It *was* the fourth cup in the space of an hour. I am grateful, really I am. I just don't *do* bed rest. It just isn't me.'

'You don't say,' he said, pausing in the stairwell to smile into her face. She smiled back and he planted a soft kiss at the corner of her mouth.

'I did think about Isaac's bar followed by dancing but I thought that might finish you off,' he said, taking the stairs again. At the bottom he pushed open the door of Ignite with one foot and carried her across the restaurant to a corner table while the staff and customers looked at them with interest. He set her down gently.

'I can actually get around by limping, you know,' she protested. He raised sarcastic eyebrows at her and she backed down with a grin. 'But Ignite is perfect.' Just knowing her well enough to see that she'd been going stir crazy was enough to melt her heart. Dinner out was an unexpected bonus.

Ignite did a great line in wine and tapas when it wasn't being a coffee lounge and, tucking into a shared platter over glasses of chilled white wine, it was easy to let herself relax in Alex's company. She let her guard take the evening off, knowing normal self-reliance would be back in charge the moment she could put her weight back on her ankle. She didn't argue at his insistence throughout the evening that she keep her foot up on the opposite chair, or at his refusal to let her walk back up the stairs to the flat when the evening was over. Yes, there was a growing closeness between them, but she was fully conscious of it, that was the most important thing here. And she should be able to move back into her own flat at the end of this week. That would put a bit of distance right back into the situation. And so surely there was absolutely no harm in feeling a little bit cared about until then.

When sleep arrived later that evening, it was in his arms.

Lara stretched deliciously, blinked her eyes open, and tried to pull her scrambled sleep-fuzzy brain together. She felt well rested for once. None of the usual hankering from her body for more sleep, which she always steadfastly ignored. No disorientation about where she was—it seemed after years of sleeping, of doing everything alone, all it took was a few nights to get used to sharing her bed with someone else. *His* bed, if she wanted to split hairs. The golden autumn sunshine slanted through the curtains and into the military order, which was only tempered a tiny bit by the items of her own clothing slung randomly over the back of a chair. She turned her head to the left then and realised Alex wasn't there. His side of the bed had the covers thrown back.

Frowning, she leaned up on one elbow. The flat was quiet. None of the clattering from the kitchen that signified Alex making one of his endless cups of coffee. And it occurred to her that the room was unusually bright. She was used to scrambling around in the semi-darkness when she got up in the mornings. And then, as her mind began to focus properly, her stomach kicked in with a hideous lurching sensation. The kind of lurch that came when you overslept on the morning of an exam or missed a really important meeting. The kind of lurch that she never experienced because Lara Connor did not *do* lateness or poor organisational skills. Ever.

She was across the bed in one swift scrambling movement, grabbing at Alex's alarm clock with a flash of horror. Two facts careered madly through her brain: it was five minutes shy of ten o'clock and someone had switched the alarm off. Right about now she should be standing, perfectly groomed, behind the counter of her shop greeting the morning customers with a smile. Instead her hair was in its first-thing fright-wig mode, there was sleep in the corners of her eyes and her hard-won clientele would be greeted by a locked door and a 'Closed' sign.

She'd thrown herself out of the bed, plonked both feet to the floor and stood up before she remembered the previous day's injury. She yelped in pain and hopped back onto the bed, one hand clamped to her throbbing ankle, the other scraping through her hair as she put two and two together.

Alex had obviously, without so much as a whisper in her direction, taken a unilateral decision to let her have a lie-in, probably because of some personal-trainer opinion about resting injured limbs for *days*. Clearly it would be perfectly fine for him with the balance of his trust fund as a cushion to take a morning off work whenever he felt like it. She, on the other hand, had no back-up plan worth beans. Did he not understand she had a *business* to run?

Limping out to the kitchen, she found no trace of either him or Poppy, although his enormous coffee mug was upended in the sink.

She also found no trace of the keys to the shop despite turning the kitchen counter upside down. Her frantic call to his mobile phone went straight to voice mail and the only explanation was so unthinkable that she came to a shocked standstill in the middle of the room.

Alex wouldn't have opened the shop, would he?

The sign on the door read 'Open' and she could see through the glass door that Alex was standing behind the counter at the back of the shop.

'What the hell is going on?' She stormed through the door on the wave of anger and frustration that had built to a crest during the taxi ride. 'Who the hell do you think you are, opening my shop without even asking me? Taking my keys? Letting me oversleep?'

His welcoming smile disappeared like smoke.

'Thank you, Alex, for looking after the shop for me while I took a much-needed rest,' he said loudly. 'You twisted your ankle yesterday. That kind of injury needs to be rested, not squashed into a four-inch heel.'

He glanced downward at that moment to see she was wearing a pair of soft leather ballet flats and made a backtracking chuffing sound through his nose. 'Well, I see you've at least decided to be sensible about footwear,' he conceded.

She didn't bother to enlighten him that she'd tried half a dozen heeled pairs before admitting to herself that limping was a whole lot easier and less attention-grabbing in flat shoes. No way was she just passing across the upper hand. He was the one in the wrong here.

'But you should still be resting up,' he carried on. 'You never take a break. You're always on the go. And since I don't have any training sessions today, I thought I'd help you out. I've sold half a dozen pairs of those knickers that look like shorts and one of those sets of pyjamas.' He spoke with the triumphant air of someone who'd just discovered a natural flair for sales that would floor Alan Sugar.

'Without even *asking* me?' she snapped incredulously. 'Would it have *killed* you to ask me my opinion before you took over my business? You didn't even leave a note, for Pete's sake.'

'I was trying to do you a favour,' he said. He waved a hand around at the shop floor. 'The place didn't spontaneously combust just because you weren't at the helm for *one bloody hour*. I am not a total imbecile.'

His voice had suddenly taken on an icy cold and even more clipped tone than usual. She realised with a jolt of surprise how angry he actually was. It filtered through to her one-track work-obsessed mind that she might be overreacting here the teeniest bit, and she made a too-late effort to curb her tongue.

'It's my business, Alex,' she said, attempting to explain. 'It's all I've got.'

'So it's fine for me to take you out to dinner and pamper you a bit but when it comes to trusting me with something that actually *matters* to you, you revert to control freak,' he snapped, walking out from behind the counter and storming past her towards the door. 'Since this place is the only thing that's remotely important to you, I'll leave you to get the hell on with it.'

He was out of the shop before she had time to say

anything else and slammed the door behind him so hard she was surprised the plate-glass window didn't shatter.

It took ten minutes to reorganise the counter back to her own liking instead of in his right-angles–lined-up obsessive military neatness. Ten minutes during which seething and self-righteousness gradually gave way to niggling doubt about who was in the wrong here and who exactly had overstepped the mark in terms of reasonable behaviour.

She couldn't fail to see that he'd made a careful list of the items he'd sold, and when she did a quick check of the till it balanced perfectly. He'd managed without a hitch. When you got right down to it, he was trying to do something nice for her, looking out for her. And of course he was confused as hell because last night she'd allowed that without complaint. But then it hadn't been about her beloved lingerie business, had it? Big difference between letting him spoil her with a meal and letting him take the reins of the most important thing in her life. The alarm bells that had started ringing yesterday when he'd helped her home after she'd twisted her ankle had gone into overdrive and she'd acted without thinking, concerned only with looking after the safe and secure little world she'd built for herself, believing that only *she* was capable of doing that.

She'd overreacted. He'd been spot on when he'd called her a control freak. And now she had to find a way of climbing down.

She managed until lunchtime. Her interim attempts to get hold of Alex went straight to voice mail and even a short rush of late-morning customers failed to stop the unhappy churning in her stomach. Her mind constantly picked at the situation, at her own behaviour. A bolt of ivory silk had been delivered for Izzy's wedding dress and she found herself staring at it miserably. Had she actually been daydreaming about having a future like that herself? Only now did she see how far beyond her that was, how unsuited she was with her present attitude to being part of a proper couple. If she couldn't relinquish control and put her trust in someone else, how could she ever hope to share her life with someone?

She ran her shop, her life, her world in her own way. The problem was, she wasn't really sure that was what she wanted, not anymore.

The first step towards change would be to apologise, of course. If he would listen after the spoilt-brat way she'd behaved towards him. And unfortunately, it became slowly clear to her that the only way to climb down and convince him she wasn't just talking the talk but was actually serious would be to put her money where her mouth was. Or, more accurately, her shop.

If anything proved to her that she was in too deep here it was this one tiny action of turning the sign on the glass door of the shop to read 'Closed' when it was currently two o'clock in the afternoon. Three hours' business time left and she was sacrificing a chunk of it to sort out her personal life. She who didn't even *have* a personal life, let alone one whose importance interfered with shop opening hours. She did it anyway.

There was a moment where she faltered as she walked past the door of her own studio flat on the fire station stairs, a floor below Poppy's flat. A couple of weeks ago and everything had been so straightforward. The pop-up shop had consumed her every waking thought; she'd been utterly focused. She couldn't have imagined anything distracting her from that. And now look at her, back here when she could be working, because when it came right down to it she just couldn't let the situation lie.

Alex was in the kitchen at the flat, the open laptop on the table displaying some kind of fitness website. He glanced up at her in amazement.

'What are you doing back here?'

'We need to talk,' she said, putting her keys and bag down on the table and sitting down. His face was completely inscrutable, which didn't help at all. She had no clue if she was in with a chance of turning the situation around.

'You've shut the shop? In the middle of the day? Bloody hell, call CNN,' he said. She let that slide. She deserved it.

She looked down at her fingers.

'I may have overreacted,' she began. 'A little.'

His face didn't change in the slightest.

'What the hell happened to you that you can't even let someone lend you a hand for a morning?' he said. 'I've never known such a control freak.'

'It's not about being a control freak,' she protested. 'It's about being professional.'

'It's about having a chip on your shoulder about accepting help.'

She bit back the indignant denials that rose to her lips. She could deny it all she wanted but her behaviour today had spoken volumes. To herself as well as to him.

'I'm just not used to delegating and the shock of waking up and finding that you'd gone ahead and opened up without even asking what I thought—'

'What exactly are you trying to say?' he snapped, making it perfectly clear that edging around an apology simply wasn't going to cut the mustard.

'I'm trying to say I'm sorry,' she blurted out. 'I know you were trying to help. I'm just not used to people doing that.' She paused, and then corrected, 'I'm not used to *letting* people do that.'

'You don't say.'

She put her elbows on the table and pushed her hands into her hair, looking down at the scrubbed wood table top.

'Accepting help from people, handing over responsibility for things, that isn't something I do lightly,' she said. 'I promised myself a long time ago that I'd make my own success in life, that I'd get where I wanted to be on my own, without having to rely on anyone else's input.' She shrugged. 'I may have become a bit rabid about that.'

A smile twitched at the corner of his lips and her heart turned softly over.

'You think?'

She smiled back.

'I made the mistake too many times when I was growing up. Of trusting people, thinking I knew where I was and then having everything change again.'

'You mean your mother?' His gaze sharpened and he reached out and shut the lid of the laptop. 'I do get that, Lara. It must have been tough when you were small, but when you talked about it I kind of got the impression that things were much more settled after you were fostered.'

Of course he had. It was exactly the impression she'd intended to give. If only it had been that simple. Straight into care, touch base and straight out again to the perfect foster family. Accepted and loved. Integrated easily at school. Grew up well-adjusted with lasting supportive family ties. This was the real world though, and she'd quickly seen that life just wasn't that warm and fuzzy. Verbalising the reality didn't come easily but she forced herself.

'I gave you the airbrushed version,' she said. 'The bits I think are worth remembering.' She held a hand up in response to his questioning expression. 'You're not the only one with baggage, Alex. We've all got it. We all have to find our own way to deal with it. For me, it's about being in control, about making my own decisions and building a secure life. And for a long time that's been something that I've done on my own. I'm way past believing that anyone else is going to do it for me.'

She took a deep breath.

'I told you my mother couldn't look after me,' she said. 'I spent some time in a children's home and then I was fostered.' She paused. 'And then when that didn't work it was back into the care system until I was fostered again.' She managed a strangled laugh. 'And again. Unfortunately there must have been something about me that meant I didn't fit in. It takes time to settle in with new people and I'd just about start to get a handle on it, then it wouldn't work out and back I'd go. It was so unsettling. I was constantly changing schools, as fast as I made any friends it felt like I moved on again. Eventually I gave up trying.'

A surge of sympathy tugged at Alex's chest as he imagined her as a little kid being shifted from one household to the next. And something else, the oddest thing: the sensation of things falling into place, of *understanding*. Because once he'd been a kid of five arriving at boarding school loaded down with a trunk and a tuck box and rejection. That sense of not being wanted hollowed you out deep inside. He'd been able to fill the gap before long, with friends, with the teachers and pastoral assistants at school. Then later with his comrades in the army. He'd been lucky in that at least there had been continuity for him: he'd stayed at the same school throughout his childhood, had made lifelong enduring friends. Isaac was a case in point. For Alex, it had become his home and family. Lara hadn't even had that. Little wonder that she was so determined now to go it alone.

'It carried on until I hit my teens, backwards and forwards to this placement or that, and then one day I ended up with Bridget and her husband,' Lara said. He could hear the affection for these people in her voice. 'I stayed with them right up until I started college. That was the only place that lasted.' She gave him a rueful smile. 'By then I think the damage was done though. And there's still this niggling doubt that maybe I moved out before they could get fed up with me, and *that's* the real reason it worked with them and not the others.'

'Do you really believe that?'

She thought of Bridget's kindness, the time and effort she'd given to helping Lara settle in, and finding something she could focus on. She shook her head.

'No, I don't really believe that. It's just that for some reason the times I was sent back resonate more with me than the one time I got to stay. Like any criticism, I suppose. You always take more notice of the bad stuff—did you ever notice that?'

He stretched across the table and took her hand in his.

'By the time I went to live with Bridget I was only a couple of years away from college age. And when I found I had a flair for sewing and I could actually *make money* at it, well, that was like finding the perfect answer. If I took charge of my own life and made my own security, I'd never have to leave it. My mistake was looking for someone else to make that life for me. Thinking that I could somehow slot into someone else's perfect family. I decided I'd make my own future that no one could take away from me. There would be no more lurking fear that just as I got close to people I'd be moving on.'

'That's why you're so work-obsessed,' he said. It made perfect sense now.

'I don't see it as *obsessed*,' she said. 'I know I'm driven but it's not about making millions—it's just about making enough for me to put down some roots, so I can have some security.' She lifted her chin a little and gave him a look of triumph. 'Maybe buy a place and get settled. And it will be all the sweeter because I got there myself.'

'I get where you're coming from now,' he said. 'Your determination to do every minute little thing on your own, no matter what the cost. I can understand that. But you don't need to go it alone. Not anymore.'

She looked up at him and the expression on her face made his heart turn softly over.

'I'm sorry,' she said. 'I'm just not used to people being there for me.'

He stood up and rounded the table, pulled her to her feet and tugged her against him. She tucked her head beneath his chin as he wrapped his arms around her.

'Then get used to it,' he said.

CHAPTER ELEVEN

Evenings out on the town were a thing of the past. His growing business brought with it a new routine. Clients in the morning and boot-camp groups a couple of afternoons a week. Lara had got the go-ahead to move back into the studio flat and now they split their time between his place and hers. Normal couple. Normal *life*. October was almost at an end now, soon winter would be kicking in, but Poppy had told him she was happy for him to stay put in the flat as long as he wanted. The sense of belonging somewhere again, of having a purpose, felt like finding his way home after being cast adrift and floundering for months.

And tonight, Lara was home first. He'd had a late training session and so she'd decided to treat him to a home-cooked dinner in his own flat. He was greeted by the delicious aroma of salmon with ginger, lime and coriander. There was a green salad and chilled white wine.

'The personal training sessions are really taking off,' he said as she sat down opposite him. He poured them each a glass of wine. 'Offering a taster session for free is really working out well. I picked up another new client today, word of mouth.'

'That's great,' she said.

There was a troubled undertone to her voice that belied the breezy smile. In fact now he came to think about it, she'd been a bit detached and quiet this last couple of days. He'd assumed it was just that she was tired.

'What's up?' he said. 'Everything all right at the shop?'

Asking him about future plans made a cold little pebble of dread land in Lara's chest and she forced herself to carry on regardless. These last few weeks had been so great, for the first time in years she'd actually begun to let someone else's presence slip into her life. The temptation to just let it carry on, not questioning what it was or where it might lead, was overwhelming. Because that way she wouldn't have to run the risk of an answer she didn't want to hear.

Unfortunately the situation wouldn't allow for them to just drift along much further with no direction. The lease would be up before she knew it on the pop-up shop. Already she was halfway through. She needed to consider what her next steps should be with the business. And it wasn't just that—there was the flat to consider. She'd only intended on renting it for the duration of the shop lease and that had been done on the strength of her savings. There was no way she could afford to keep renting in Notting Hill in the long term.

'I've been thinking about the future,' she said, not looking at him. 'The pop-up shop is a really short-term lease, remember. Just until the end of November and then I'll have to ship out. Someone else will move into the premises, probably some Christmas shop or other.'

He frowned a little as he forked up some of his fish.

'OK, so what are you thinking of doing after that? Knowing you, you've probably got the next ten years mapped out.'

She took a deep breath and kept a neutral expression on her face.

OK, so he hadn't immediately leapt in with an enthusiastic torrent of suggestions of how they might proceed from here—*together*. She bit the inside of her cheek to distract herself from the surge of disappointment that brought. Just because she was making a conscious effort to take a step back from control freak didn't mean she had to flip to the other end of the scale and start working needy. He probably wasn't thinking beyond the next week or so, but his lack of future plans didn't necessarily have to have anything to do with his regard for her, right?

'That's the thing,' she said. 'I need to start thinking about where I'm going with it next.'

He tucked into the salad.

'The shop's doing well, isn't it?'

She nodded and took a sip of her wine.

'It's done really well, but it was only ever really an experiment. I need to start planning where I'm going with it next, whether I run with the retail thing and look for another shop or maybe trial internet sales on a wider scale.'

'Why not put some figures together for the different options and then we can talk it through?' he said. 'Weigh up the pros and cons.'

The long-ingrained urge to politely decline any offer of help rose to her lips just as it always did. This time she swallowed it. He was in her corner. In time sharing things with him would surely become less conscious and more natural.

'Great,' she said. And it was great. She felt more settled than she had in years, secure and happy.

As they finished the meal she stood up to make coffee and he joined her, curling his arms around her waist, kissing her neck from behind, making her so deliciously hot. She turned in his arms and he tilted her face up gently to meet his. Not fast or furious this time, no rushing. His mouth found hers and she melted against him. He picked her up and carried her down the hall to his room as if she weighed nothing at all.

Undressing her was an indulgent pleasure and Alex lingered over it, revelled in it, kissing her skin inch by silken inch until she was squirming with desire. Then he lay above her, feeling the soft curl of her arms and legs around him, binding him to her. Her soft cry of pleasure at his first thrust deep inside her thrilled him on a visceral level that drove his own arousal to an ever higher level. He plunged both hands into her hair and cradled her face as he took her, in long, slow, delicious strokes. Her china-blue eyes were wide as he looked down at her, holding his own gaze steadily, sharing every sensation with him. Feeling her writhe in ecstasy beneath him sent him careering beside her towards that shared height of pleasure.

Crazy, hot, short-term sex, this wasn't. This sex had strings. This was making love, savouring every touch, every inch of her skin. Wanting to please her more than himself. This was what it was like to let someone in.

The joy in that sensation was tinged with a gnawing edge of danger that he tried hard to ignore. Afterwards they lay sated in each other's arms and he felt her urgent grip on his shoulders slowly relax.

'I think I could get used to this,' she whispered against his hair as his breathing began to level. He could feel her own breath warm against his skin.

She settled lower, curling up into the crook of his arm,

and he felt her smile against his shoulder as she twined his fingers into her own.

'These past few weeks have been great,' she said. 'I've been on my own for so long that I'd got used to managing everything. I actually thought I liked living that way. I used to tell myself that was the best way to be—no one to answer to but myself, no one to let me down. I never thought I could have this sense of belonging—I thought it was beyond me. It's so lovely, feeling protected and looked after by you, knowing it's not just me against the world for a change.'

She leaned up on one elbow and smiled into his eyes.

'I love knowing you've got my back,' she said. 'And you know I've got yours.'

She pulled away a little so she could find his mouth and kiss him. As the words registered in his mind a hideous black sense of déjà vu stormed through his veins like ice water, picking up speed as it reached his heart.

What the hell had he been thinking?

You've got my back...and I've got yours.

The words filled him with fear as he recalled the last time he'd heard them. Private Sam Walker, now deceased. He'd been unable to save him, unable even to *find* him in the aftermath of the bomb. He'd failed to look out for him after all.

She'd come to rely on him.

Lara Connor, who relied on no one, who did everything for herself, who decided what she wanted from life and found a way to take it without enlisting anyone else's help. And in a flash of unsettling clarity it came to him. That was what he'd found most alluring about her all along. Lara was someone who could manage perfectly well without him. She didn't need him to protect her or look out for her. He had to force her to accept help, such was her level of perfect control freak. As such, the prospect of letting her down or failing her hadn't come into play. And in encouraging her to change, in pushing her to lean on him and let him look out for her, he'd ruled himself completely out of the game.

He lay rigid in the bed next to her long after she'd fallen asleep, curled up in a warm ball against his chest, wanting the façade he'd created. Desperately wanting to be that man with that perfect life—beautiful girlfriend, fledgling new business, new life all mapped out just there for the taking. Knowing he couldn't be, knowing it was all for show and that underneath the exterior he'd created so carefully that he'd actually begun to believe in it himself, he wasn't that man at all.

The revelation that now she *needed* him, that she felt protected, that she was revelling in having someone looking out for her for once, that she saw a future with him, made tendrils of cold dread begin to curl through him. He wasn't up to that challenge. The last person he'd encouraged to depend on him had died on his watch. Just what the hell had he been thinking?

There was no struggle to stay awake tonight while he waited for her to fall asleep. He lay next to her in the bed, tense with shock at his own arrogant stupidity. So determined to channel normality that he'd actually begun to *believe* in his own fiction.

Her talk this evening over dinner about the next move for her business came back to him. Her lease would be up in a matter of weeks. Was that why he'd let this get so far when he really should have known better? Because, subconsciously, he'd always seen an end point in sight to this? He'd known from their first meeting that she was here for a couple of months, no more. She'd told him, that day he'd fallen asleep in her flat, that she'd sunk her savings into this couple of months. *Couple of months.* Deep down had he believed this to be temporary? Just another longer version of his flings, commitment free? And therefore safe.

As her breathing evened, he eased his way out of the bed and moved to the kitchen, the same way he had for the past few nights.

The old single bed in Poppy's boxroom was so narrow that Lara hadn't been able to turn over without bashing herself on the wall of the boxroom. Sharing Alex's big double bed after that was pure luxury and as she surfaced from sleep somewhere in the small hours she stretched deliciously to her toes before turning over to snuggle back up to him.

His side of the bed was empty.

For a disoriented moment she wondered if she'd over-slept again and he'd got up to open the shop without asking her, like some crazy Groundhog Day rerun of the other morning. But no, the other morning the room had been light with sunshine, not pitch dark as it was now. She came awake more fully and pulled herself up onto her elbow, screwing her eyes up to read the digital clock on Alex's bedside table. A little past three in the morning. She lay for a few minutes, assuming he must be in the bathroom, or maybe getting a drink from the kitchen, but nothing. The minutes stretched ahead and she was wide awake now. Maybe he was ill.

That thought galvanised her into action and she threw the covers back and grabbed her robe from where it lay over a chair. The hallway was as dark as the bedroom. Poppy's bedroom door was closed and the bathroom was empty and silent. She padded down to the kitchen and immediately saw the slice of light cutting out beneath the closed door. She opened it and went into the room.

Alex visibly jumped as she came in. He was sitting at the table behind his laptop, a mug of coffee the size of a small bucket next to his hand, and a look on his face of pure guilt. *I'm caught,* it said. The guilt thing was so obvious that it shut out all other details as her mind searched madly for a simple explanation. What reason could a man have for sitting at his laptop in the middle of the night, sporting a guilty expression, except possibly for porn?

The instant that thought hit her brain, she marched across the room and took in his laptop screen. Not porn but the website for his new business. There was a notepad next to his hand and he was clearly working. Maybe he just couldn't sleep.

That thought in itself tripped some kind of alarm in her mind.

'What are you doing up?' she asked. 'I was worried. I thought you might be ill.'

He smiled at her.

'I just couldn't sleep. Thought I might as well get up and do something else.'

He pushed up from the table and attempted to sweep her into a hug. She batted his hands aside. Her mind was working overtime now.

She noticed with new clarity the dark shadows under his eyes as he failed to meet her gaze, shadows she'd noticed back in her flat when they first met, and like a bucket of cold water being sloshed over her she realised that those dark shadows had never really gone away. Her mind picked up other telltale details. The enormous coffee mug by his hand. The documents that strewed the table. His amazing ability to start up a business and cope with all the associated admin when she'd always felt as if she never had enough hours in the day.

'I couldn't sleep either,' she said. 'But I do what most normal people who can't sleep do at three in the morning. Warm milk and counting sheep. Whereas you've launched yourself into the working day.'

She waved a hand at the table, covered in papers, lists of figures, business card and poster samples. Her sleep-addled brain continued to make connections.

'I woke up three nights ago and you weren't there,' she said. 'It was some godforsaken small hour of the morning. I assumed you'd gone to the bathroom so I just turned over but you weren't there, were you? You were in here. Working. And your coffee addiction. On the whole, it's worse. I've never known anyone guzzle so much caffeine.'

She paused.

'This is about your nightmares, isn't it?' she said simply.

The words made Alex's stomach begin to churn.

'I'm dealing with it,' he said, clenching his hands.

'You told me you were dealing with it weeks ago,' she said. 'But staying awake isn't the answer. You're burying your head in the sand. That is *not* dealing with it.'

He sat down at the table and she tugged her silk dressing gown tighter around her and sank into the chair next to him, reached out to touch his wrist. He stared down at her hand, intended to comfort him, and shame began to climb burningly upward from his neck.

'You can't keep denying you have a problem,' she said

firmly. 'I let you fob me off last time because I thought things were getting better but by the look of it they're worse than ever.' Her smile was supportive. 'You don't need to worry,' she said. 'I'm here for you. We'll get you all the help you need.'

On the back of his fears about being able to take care of her now came this. He was a total basket case. He needed *help*. In her offer to get him support, she'd just inadvertently confirmed his failure. He was a failure as a soldier, as a comrade and friend. And if he stayed in her life, he would fail her too. She deserved better than that after the constant let-downs she'd already endured throughout her childhood. He gritted his teeth hard and forged ahead with his only option.

'This isn't going to work between us,' he said.

She was close enough for him to hear her catch her breath.

'What?' she whispered.

He pulled his arm away from her hand, stood up and backed away to lean against the kitchen counter, wanting to put distance between them now, steeling himself to go through with this, knowing it was for the best.

'I've been pretending that it could. Playing at normality,' he said. 'Kidding myself that I could work a normal relationship. Dating, supporting each other, sitting round the table eating dinner while we talk about our day. Sleeping together. All those things that *normal* people do. But all the time I've just been using it to hide reality.'

'From me?'

He shook his head and ran a hand briefly through his hair.

'Worse than that. From *me*. I've been kidding myself that I can be the man you deserve, that I can look after

you in the way you need. I'm not up to that, Lara. I'll let
you down—it's inevitable. Just a matter of time.'

'You're *dumping* me?' she said, her tone incredulous.

'A clean break is best,' he said. 'I'm not good for you,
Lara. I'm not what you need.'

She held up a hand at that and he saw anger rush to
her face.

'Don't you dare!' she snapped. 'Don't you *dare* spin
me that it's-not-you-it's-me line. I should have listened
to my instincts when I twisted my ankle. You let me
think I could *count* on you. Have you any idea how hard
it was for me to accept that? And now you're just saying you didn't mean it after all? I should never have let
this get off the ground. I mean, have I not learned *anything*?' She tipped her head back and laughed sarcasti-
cally at the ceiling.

'It's not a line.'

'How can this *possibly* be about you?' she asked him
then. She waved a hand at him. 'I mean, look at you—
you've got half of Notting Hill's women salivating after
you. You're smart, brave, funny, gorgeous.'

He was shaking his head.

'It *is* about me. I can't be the person you need me to
be.' He lifted his hands in an all-encompassing gesture.
'None of this is real,' he said. 'This thing we have. Relationship. Whatever you want to call it. I thought I was
doing such a great job. I thought that by going through
the motions I could actually *be* normal, but it doesn't
work. It's all a façade. I'm not the person you think I am
and I'm not right for you.'

The words fell on Lara like stones. In other words,
she didn't fit with him. And as a knock-on effect, she
supposed, with his sister or his friends. And he clearly

thought he could spare her a rundown of her personal failings to live up by blaming himself.

She bit the inside of her cheek to stop the burning sensation at the back of her throat from turning into anything more obvious. Funny how the age-old survival techniques kicked right back in. It felt as if she were twelve again, another foster home not working out, holding her head up high as she packed her things up, all ready to move on and insisting to herself that she didn't care; *she didn't care*. It wasn't about *her,* oh, no, it was about finding the right situation, the right family setting for her needs, the right *fit*.

When it came right down to it, none of his excuses really mattered. At best, even if she accepted what he was saying, it meant he'd never been straight with her. If manufacturing some ludicrous normality and hiding his sleep loss was preferable to just being honest with her, then he had a very different view of how important this relationship was. Whatever the reasons were, she wasn't right for him. She didn't want or need to hear any more excuses, in the same way as she hadn't wanted or needed to hear the explanations throughout her childhood. She wasn't a good fit, either now or back then, and she never should have kidded herself that she could be.

She stood up from the table and pushed the chair carefully back into place.

'I'm not bothered, Alex,' she said. She didn't raise her voice. She dug deep for all the dignity she could muster. 'I don't *need* to talk about this. I don't need any of your excuses. It was good while it lasted but my work has always come first. No big deal.'

She backed away from the table and out of the door and then he heard her practically sprint downstairs to her own flat. He was on his feet before he'd given it a moment's thought, ready to run after her. He hadn't reckoned on this. Hadn't thought for a second she would make it about *her*. This was *his* screw-up. How could she possibly believe this could be due to some failing of hers?

Then instinct was pushed away by reason. This was for the best; he was letting her off the hook, doing her a favour. Clean break, as he'd said to her. He could go down that hallway, bang on her door and talk with her all night, but the conclusion would be the same. This couldn't continue. He'd been a fool to let it go on as long as it had. He simply couldn't have people relying on him and she really was better off without him. The only way forward now was on his own. He really should have known that from the start.

CHAPTER TWELVE

'How are you holding up?'

Lara could feel Izzy's eyes looking down on her from where she stood on one of the old second-hand dining chairs in the middle of her studio flat. Putting her heart and soul into making a wedding dress, the epitome of a happy-ever-after, wasn't the automatic choice of therapy for a broken heart, but she was fine. She could do this. She was a *professional*. Faking a breezy 'I'm over him' wasn't that much of a challenge, she found. But then again she was a past master of toughing things out with a brave face.

'I'm absolutely fine,' she said, around a mouthful of pins. 'It's for the best. I'm not cut out to be one of a couple. I never have been.'

Perhaps if she said that often enough to herself and everyone else, it might actually start to make her feel better. Some time this century might be nice.

Wedding-dress fittings from now would take place in her own little flat, a venue change from that first talk she'd had with Izzy about dress styles, up in Poppy's living room, champagne in hand, surrounded by her new friends. Lara hadn't set foot in the flat upstairs since things had ended with Alex. No matter that he was away somewhere right now, accompanying Isaac at the last minute on one of his endless bar scouting trips, running away from his problems. Apparently a flight of stairs wasn't enough distance for him; he'd decided to leave the country rather than run the gauntlet of bumping into her in the hallway. Her stomach gave its now familiar miserable churn as she failed yet again to squash him from her mind. Somehow that was the worst part of all, the lingering concern for him, reminding her just how far she'd fallen for him, just how much she cared.

Poppy's flat and the friends who shared it were as much a part of what was lost to her as he was. Her stupidity in thinking that misfit Lara Connor could fit in here, in rich Notting Hill, now amazed her. She should have known better. All that was left now was to see out the lease on the pop-up shop and this flat, and to finish Izzy's dress, of course.

She'd had to bring the big guns back into play. The old tactics she'd learned as a kid, shunted back and forth, never feeling settled or wanted. Withdrawal into her own company and refocusing on the one thing that had brought her answers: work. She'd committed to making Izzy's dress, and although she longed to run for the hills she was also a professional who took pride in her work. She wouldn't let Izzy down. Shame she wouldn't see the wedding itself though; she'd be long gone by then.

She took a step back, hands on hips, and surveyed the gown, currently pinned and tacked together so that she could easily adjust seams. Even half finished, it looked great.

'Oh, Iz.' Poppy sighed from the sofa. 'It's just gorgeous.'

Glamour. Excitement. Freedom. Full-on whirlwind distraction from the real world. When you got down to it, that was what Isaac's chain of bars was all about, providing his clientele with the ultimate distraction through sophisticated entertainment and leisure. *That* was what Alex needed. That was what he should have been aiming for all along. No ties. No responsibilities. For the first few days away, living it up in Isaac's world, the relief at relinquishing accountability for anyone else was overwhelming. No need to worry about letting Lara down, or anyone else for that matter.

She was better off without him.

For the first few days, he'd been convinced that he'd done the right thing by walking away. He'd thrown himself with abandon into a few all-nighters at the clubs, surrounded by pretty girls. Had told himself that he was having a *great time.*

Unfortunately there was only one direction to go when you were at the pinnacle of *great time.*

Without his carefully honed sleep pattern, the nightmares began to creep back in. Last night had been the most gut-wrenching, hideous one yet, leaving him cold and shaking in his hotel room. It seemed there was no end to it, no way of putting the past behind him.

Lara had made him feel as if he could conquer anything.

He kept coming across that thought unexpectedly, popping up from nowhere, despite his efforts to keep her out of his mind. The thought of her made his stomach clench with misery. Before he'd met her he'd been stuck in limbo, no clue how to move forward, his mind constantly occupied by his past. Her reassurance and help had got his business off the ground, had given his life some focus again. His nightmares might still have plagued him, but they'd felt somehow more manageable because he'd had a new life to anchor himself to.

Lara had had confidence in him when he'd had none left in himself, and without her encouragement, her endless optimism, he was utterly lost. He'd tagged along on this trip with Isaac at the last minute, anything to get away and maybe get some perspective. He'd called his fitness clients and told them he'd be gone for a few weeks. Yet living it up and playing the field wasn't the answer and he had absolutely no idea what was. And finally black despair surged through him as he fumbled his wallet from his pocket.

He sat on the edge of his bed in the nondescript hotel room and flipped through until he found the card. Just to look at it, not necessarily to *call* the number on it. A military charity, offering help for soldiers under stress. He'd taken the number out of politeness when he'd left hospital months ago, brushing off the slightest mention of PTSD, never intending to call it, never believing he would need to. To call that number would be to admit defeat, to acknowledge that he couldn't do this on his own.

He picked up his phone.

He'd flown back to London alone, declining Isaac's offer to accompany him on the second leg of the trip. The flat was exactly as he'd left it, his room tidy to military standards of precision. The comfort that had once given him seemed to have diminished a little now. Lara had come with endless *stuff* that began to seep into his room. Clothes left hanging over chairs, cosmetics on the dresser. He'd had to fight the urge to tidy up after her, but now he kind of missed the mess.

He dumped his bag and headed straight to Portobello

Road, determined to give this his best shot. He knew now that honesty was the only path open to him. By the time he'd finished she might be congratulating herself on her lucky escape. He came to a standstill outside the little shop with the pink and black sign, composing himself. Well, here went everything. Hadn't that been one of the most attractive things about Lara? That her reactions were never predictable? And she was used to being on her own, that much he knew. None of it gave him much confidence in the outcome. But damn it, he had to *try*.

He pushed open the door of the shop and went in. The usual floral scent of the French soaps and perfumes she stocked smacked him immediately between the eyes, the way it always did. Lara was at the back of the shop behind the little counter, gift-wrapping something pink and silky for a middle-aged woman, who glanced his way with interest. He saw Lara stiffen almost imperceptibly as she saw him, her blue eyes widening, and then her inscrutable expression locked into place. Not a single clue as to what his reception might be. As he approached she handed over one of her signature pink and black bags with the black silk ribbon handles to her customer and turned to him.

'Yes, sir?' She gave him a breezy smile. 'How can I help you? Looking for something for a girlfriend? You look like the quick throwaway-fling type. Let me guess— something red with peepholes.' Her just-served customer was looking on with interest and Lara swept past Alex to the front of the shop to hold the door open for her. 'I'm sorry but I don't think I'll be able to help,' she called back to him over her shoulder. 'I'm not sure what you were expecting but that kind of thing *really isn't me*.'

The emphasis on those last few words made it crystal

clear that if he'd thought talking her round was going to be a piece of cake, he was sadly mistaken. She closed the door behind her customer, turned the sign around to read 'Closed', and turned back to him.

'Make it quick,' she said. 'Say what you've got to say. Time is money. Every minute I close the shop I'm losing sales.'

'I came to say I'm sorry,' he said.

He saw her press her lips together.

'For what?' she said. 'For letting me think we actually had some kind of relationship there, letting me buy into all of that, when it was all for show?'

He closed his eyes briefly.

'It wasn't all for show. The way I feel about you was and is not just for show. I'm sorry for hiding my problems from you but I truly thought I could deal with them on my own. And you have to understand that, in my family, throughout my life, that's the way it's been done. As far back as I can remember, emotional outbursts have been a sign of weakness. By the time I was seven years old I'd worked out that crying only made my father angry—it certainly didn't elicit any sympathy or affection. Soldiers don't cry. They don't show emotion.'

She was watching him steadily. He had no idea if any of this was counting for anything at all with her. He crossed the shop towards the counter, took a breath and turned back to her. She was watching him steadily.

'I thought I could put the past behind me and have this fantastic life with you,' he said. '*That* was the problem. I was kidding myself that I could actually do that. On my own, without help from anyone else. I thought if I lived a normal life with you, starting a new business, moving on, pretty soon it would become exactly that.'

'Pretending things are normal won't make them normal,' she said, her voice carefully neutral. She walked slowly across the shop towards him, her arms folded defensively across her body. 'You can't just gloss over the bad stuff and expect it to go away.'

'I know that now,' he said. 'It was partly my pride. I just couldn't bear your suggestion that I get help. You have to understand that was the last thing I wanted to hear. I'd spent so long denying I had a problem that agreeing to get help was unthinkable. I thought I'd rather manage on my own than admit that. I decided to throw myself into partying with Isaac and I lasted less than a week. I don't want that life. But if I'm ever going to have more than that I have to face up to my past. I realise that now.'

He held her gaze carefully and a tug of sympathy pulled at Lara's heart. Yet still she steeled herself.

'Have you any idea what a big deal it was to let you into my life?' she asked him quietly. 'How much that cost me? I've never been able to take my eye off the ball and relax with someone, not since I was a kid. I'd had too many times, you see, where I'd done that, where I'd put my trust in someone, when I thought I could put down roots and be part of a family. And then the whole thing would come tumbling down around me.

'That's why I don't like to rely on other people. I've never *had* anyone to rely on. Whenever I thought I was settling in somewhere, or I got used to a new school or made a friend, before I knew it I'd be swept back into care and the whole damn thing would start all over again with another family. I just...wasn't a good fit.' She held her head high and carried on boldly, 'I made up my mind a long time ago that I'd make my own life, that I'd work hard and get my own security without having to look to anyone else's help to get me there. I knew I wouldn't let myself down. And then you came along and made me rethink all of that. And for you to just walk away from it as if it meant nothing...' she caught her breath '...that was the worst thing that could happen to me.'

She sank into the chair next to the dressing screen. Just what did he expect from her? How could he expect her to give this another try when he'd messed with her trust, that thing that was so difficult for her to give?

'There were three of us in the vehicle,' he said then, and her fingers clenched on the arms of the chair. She turned slowly to look up at him in stunned surprise, understanding what he was about to tell her.

She could pick up the tiniest falter in his clipped deep voice and her heart turned over in spite of the way she was trying to steel it against him.

'Alex, you don't need to put yourself through this,' she said. 'I don't need to hear this stuff. It's not relevant anymore.'

'I want you to understand,' he said, his expression steady. 'I don't want any more secrets. There were three of us. Driver, another soldier, and me. Same kind of journey taken countless times, no big difference about that day, nothing that made it stand out.' He shrugged. 'My memories of the bomb are sketchy. I remember a sense of building pressure, as if I could feel the explosion coming from beneath us before it really hit. I remember the smoke, the smell of explosives burning at the back of my throat. My eyes stung. And the disorientation, that was the most hideous part. I couldn't find the others. I couldn't see. I was staggering around. It was chaos.'

'It must have been terrifying.'

'It was. But at the same time it was no more than I'd

signed up for. I knew the risks. We all did. I went into it with my eyes open. And I wasn't about to have some kind of meltdown after the event. Not when I still had *my* life, that would have been a mockery of the soldier who lost his.'

He looked down at the floor.

'Private Sam Walker, his name was. The soldier who was killed.'

There was a long pause before he said any more and when he did she could hear the strain in his voice.

'It was his first tour and sometimes it takes time to adjust. Suddenly it isn't a training exercise anymore, it's the real thing and people...well, some people struggle, that's all. If I became aware of that I always tried to step in where I could, give some kind of encouragement. He'd...well, he'd had some problems and I told him I'd look out for him. That I had his back.'

He drew in a rasping breath and at last he looked up at her. His grey eyes held a tortured expression that made her heart ache for him.

'When you said that to me the other night, about having my back, it brought it all rushing back. I panicked. That's why I backed away so quickly, why I wouldn't discuss it with you or listen to reason. That's what I meant when I said it was about me not being what you need. I was determined to get well in record time after the bomb. I pushed myself like crazy in rehab. I told you I was handling it myself, that I had it under control, that it was improving, and I meant all of those things when I said them.' He shrugged. 'I think maybe I was trying to convince myself as much as you. And I know I should have got some help but I was ashamed.'

She shook her head, but he talked over her, as though if he stopped talking now he might never revisit this.

'I felt so *weak*,' he groaned, his head tilting up at the ceiling as he ran a shaky hand through his hair. 'I was an exemplary soldier, Lara. I was determined to better my father and I'd pushed myself up the ranks with sheer hard graft, I wanted to prove that I wasn't just there because of the family name. Without all of that I had no idea who the hell I was anymore, and I certainly didn't feel like I was good enough for someone as lovely as you. I got off lightly, Lara. The driver suffered terrible injuries and Sam was killed. I was the most senior person in that vehicle and there was nothing I could do for either of them.'

He was shaking all over now, both his hands clutched at the sides of his head. She was up from the chair before she knew what she was doing, pulling him tightly against her. She felt him grip her tightly, his breath heaving.

'How could I possibly trust myself to look after you when I'd failed so hideously?' His broken whisper was hot against her neck.

'You didn't fail,' she said, holding him tight. 'You didn't plant that bomb. None of what happened was your fault.'

She continued to hold him, feeling the tension in his shoulders slowly relax.

'I can't sort this out on my own,' he said after a minute, his voice muffled. 'And I know I threw your offer of support back in your face but I'm asking you to reconsider.'

She disengaged herself from his embrace and took a careful step back.

'What's changed?' she said. She searched his face. 'Why should I believe this isn't just you talking the talk and then necking off to swig espresso and pop caffeine pills?'

'Because I've got help this time,' he said. He looked away from her while he tugged a wad of paperwork from the pocket of his jacket and handed it to her. She took it and scanned it.

'A military charity?' she said.

'They run a helpline. Support for ex-servicemen who are suffering from stress. The dreams, the anxiety, they're common PTSD symptoms. I'm going to take counselling, whatever they can offer me to deal with it. No more pretending I'm improving by avoiding sleep. I know it's not going to be easy, and I'm not asking you to give me an answer right away. I just couldn't bear to have you thinking this was somehow down to some shortfall of *yours*. I'm the one with the problem here, not you.' He reached across and took her hand in his. 'I want to be with you. But I still don't feel like I'm good enough for that.'

Accepting you had a problem, wasn't that the first step to recovery?

She looked at him.

'I don't need rescuing, or looking after, Alex, so you can quit thinking I have any need for you to do that. I've done perfectly well by myself all this time. If we're going to be together then what I want is to be part of a team for once. To not be on my own. But that means we give it our best shot, the bad stuff and the good stuff included, not some stupid idea of what you think it should be like where I'm wrapped in cotton wool and you hide anything from me that you think I won't like.'

'Is that a yes?'

A tentative grin touched his lips.

'It's not as simple as that.' She'd had a good dose of

reality these last few days since he'd gone. It had made her refocus on her business plans and ambitions. 'Even if it was a yes, I'll be moving out in a few weeks. I've no idea what my plans are next. I need to give that some serious thought.'

'Move in with me at the flat,' he said immediately, grabbing both her hands in his. 'At least for now. Poppy won't mind—I know she won't. She's loved having you around. I know it all sounds like our plans are short term but that's just logistics. I'm in this for the long haul if you are. If you can give me a second chance. No secrets.'

That he'd been open with her about his past touched her deeply. That couldn't have been easy after denying it so vehemently to everyone including himself. And it still wasn't going to be rainbows and butterflies, at least for the time being. But, hell, when had her life ever been that?

She squeezed his hands. Maybe in each other they could finally find the security they both needed.

'OK,' she said at last, and then she was pulled into his arms. Her stomach melted as he kissed and kissed her.

'With one condition,' she said, coming up for air. 'No boot camp for me. Ever.'

He smiled down at her.

'Done.'

* * * * *

*If you loved this book,
make sure you catch the rest of the incredible*
THE FLAT IN NOTTING HILL *miniseries!*

*THE MORNING AFTER THE NIGHT BEFORE
by Nikki Logan, available August 2014*

*SLEEPING WITH THE SOLDIER
by Charlotte Phillips, available September 2014*

*YOUR BED OR MINE?
by Joss Wood, available October 2014*

*ENEMIES WITH BENEFITS
by Louisa George, available November 2014*

Mills & Boon® Hardback

September 2014

ROMANCE

The Housekeeper's Awakening	Sharon Kendrick
More Precious than a Crown	Carol Marinelli
Captured by the Sheikh	Kate Hewitt
A Night in the Prince's Bed	Chantelle Shaw
Damaso Claims His Heir	Annie West
Changing Constantinou's Game	Jennifer Hayward
The Ultimate Revenge	Victoria Parker
Tycoon's Temptation	Trish Morey
The Party Dare	Anne Oliver
Sleeping with the Soldier	Charlotte Phillips
All's Fair in Lust & War	Amber Page
Dressed to Thrill	Bella Frances
Interview with a Tycoon	Cara Colter
Her Boss by Arrangement	Teresa Carpenter
In Her Rival's Arms	Alison Roberts
Frozen Heart, Melting Kiss	Ellie Darkins
After One Forbidden Night...	Amber McKenzie
Dr Perfect on Her Doorstep	Lucy Clark

MEDICAL

A Secret Shared...	Marion Lennox
Flirting with the Doc of Her Dreams	Janice Lynn
The Doctor Who Made Her Love Again	Susan Carlisle
The Maverick Who Ruled Her Heart	Susan Carlisle

Mills & Boon® Large Print

September 2014

ROMANCE

The Only Woman to Defy Him	Carol Marinelli
Secrets of a Ruthless Tycoon	Cathy Williams
Gambling with the Crown	Lynn Raye Harris
The Forbidden Touch of Sanguardo	Julia James
One Night to Risk it All	Maisey Yates
A Clash with Cannavaro	Elizabeth Power
The Truth About De Campo	Jennifer Hayward
Expecting the Prince's Baby	Rebecca Winters
The Millionaire's Homecoming	Cara Colter
The Heir of the Castle	Scarlet Wilson
Twelve Hours of Temptation	Shoma Narayanan

HISTORICAL

Unwed and Unrepentant	Marguerite Kaye
Return of the Prodigal Gilvry	Ann Lethbridge
A Traitor's Touch	Helen Dickson
Yield to the Highlander	Terri Brisbin
Return of the Viking Warrior	Michelle Styles

MEDICAL

Waves of Temptation	Marion Lennox
Risk of a Lifetime	Caroline Anderson
To Play with Fire	Tina Beckett
The Dangers of Dating Dr Carvalho	Tina Beckett
Uncovering Her Secrets	Amalie Berlin
Unlocking the Doctor's Heart	Susanne Hampton

Mills & Boon® Hardback
October 2014

ROMANCE

An Heiress for His Empire	Lucy Monroe
His for a Price	Caitlin Crews
Commanded by the Sheikh	Kate Hewitt
The Valquez Bride	Melanie Milburne
The Uncompromising Italian	Cathy Williams
Prince Hafiz's Only Vice	Susanna Carr
A Deal Before the Altar	Rachael Thomas
Rival's Challenge	Abby Green
The Party Starts at Midnight	Lucy King
Your Bed or Mine?	Joss Wood
Turning the Good Girl Bad	Avril Tremayne
Breaking the Bro Code	Stefanie London
The Billionaire in Disguise	Soraya Lane
The Unexpected Honeymoon	Barbara Wallace
A Princess by Christmas	Jennifer Faye
His Reluctant Cinderella	Jessica Gilmore
One More Night with Her Desert Prince...	Jennifer Taylor
From Fling to Forever	Avril Tremayne

MEDICAL

It Started with No Strings...	Kate Hardy
Flirting with Dr Off-Limits	Robin Gianna
Dare She Date Again?	Amy Ruttan
The Surgeon's Christmas Wish	Annie O'Neil

Mills & Boon® Large Print
October 2014

ROMANCE

Ravelli's Defiant Bride	Lynne Graham
When Da Silva Breaks the Rules	Abby Green
The Heartbreaker Prince	Kim Lawrence
The Man She Can't Forget	Maggie Cox
A Question of Honour	Kate Walker
What the Greek Can't Resist	Maya Blake
An Heir to Bind Them	Dani Collins
Becoming the Prince's Wife	Rebecca Winters
Nine Months to Change His Life	Marion Lennox
Taming Her Italian Boss	Fiona Harper
Summer with the Millionaire	Jessica Gilmore

HISTORICAL

Scars of Betrayal	Sophia James
Scandal's Virgin	Louise Allen
An Ideal Companion	Anne Ashley
Surrender to the Viking	Joanna Fulford
No Place for an Angel	Gail Whitiker

MEDICAL

200 Harley Street: Surgeon in a Tux	Carol Marinelli
200 Harley Street: Girl from the Red Carpet	Scarlet Wilson
Flirting with the Socialite Doc	Melanie Milburne
His Diamond Like No Other	Lucy Clark
The Last Temptation of Dr Dalton	Robin Gianna
Resisting Her Rebel Hero	Lucy Ryder

MILLS & BOON®

Why shop at millsandboon.co.uk?

Each year, thousands of romance readers find their perfect read at millsandboon.co.uk. That's because we're passionate about bringing you the very best romantic fiction. Here are some of the advantages of shopping at www.millsandboon.co.uk:

* **Get new books first**—you'll be able to buy your favourite books one month before they hit the shops

* **Get exclusive discounts**—you'll also be able to buy our specially created monthly collections, with up to 50% off the RRP

* **Find your favourite authors**—latest news, interviews and new releases for all your favourite authors and series on our website, plus ideas for what to try next

* **Join in**—once you've bought your favourite books, don't forget to register with us to rate, review and join in the discussions

Visit **www.millsandboon.co.uk**
for all this and more today!